the rookie and the writer

ASHLYNNE KRISTINE

For anyone who has ever thought "Hm, we need more red-heads
falling in love"
Enjoy.

content warnings

Please note this book contains sexually explicit material.

scottie

"You may now kiss the bride," the officiant said.

Everyone in attendance whooped as Case—my best friend and our team captain—grabbed his newly appointed wife and dipped her back. But not before I saw the giant grin on Basil's face as she wrapped her arms over his shoulders. Now I was a sensitive man, I had no shame in that and it wasn't a secret amongst our teammates, but I was shocked when I looked over at Townes and saw a stray tear rolling down his cheek. Our team's former goalie—and my other best friend despite what he may say—was not a crier. In fact, the most emotion I'd seen out of him was when he laughed so hard he pulled a muscle.

I sniffled and threw my arms over him as my head settled on his shoulder, a tear darkened the blue fabric of his suit.

"I love weddings," I said.

"And I'd love some personal space," he mumbled as he tried to shrug me off, but I held firm, knowing he needed comfort. "Seriously, can you get off?"

I nodded and patted his back as I pulled away. "If you ever get overcome with emotions again and need another hug, just let me know, I'm always here for you."

Townes shook his head as if he was actually rejecting the thought of my company, but I knew him better than that. Despite his grumpy exterior he didn't mind putting up with my shit, and I knew it had to do with the fact that I was Hayley's favorite uncle—besides him of course. That little nine-year-old had him wrapped around his finger.

Case finally pulled away from Basil and wrapped her hand in his before they walked back down the aisle. Family and friends still cheered as they made their way to the door. Once they were out of sight, everyone started filtering out and headed toward the reception area. The cold wind shook the huge windows as we walked, and at that moment I was ecstatic I packed the biggest jacket I owned. Winter in Breckinridge was brutal but beautiful. I could see why they wanted to get married here.

Townes and I followed the crowd where we eventually split. Townes walked over to his wife, Hollis, and I was left alone to dwell on the glaring fact that I was alone. Townes had Hollis, Case had Basil, and I had a leftover cheese quesadilla waiting for me at home.

It sucked.

I had been in a dry spell for a whole month, and I was pretty sure my dick had gone into hibernation from underuse. I went from the most eligible bachelor in the Denver metro to another dude you'd find on the street. It started at Al's—the bar Hollis used to work at before her and Townes got hitched. I walked up to a pretty blonde, paid her a few compliments before I offered to pay for her beer. All was going well until I invited her back to the table and she declined. I took it like a man, if a woman said *"no"* I wasn't going to push for a different answer, but my ego took a huge hit. I left the bar shortly after and hyperfixated on that interaction for three days to figure out what went wrong, but I could never figure it out.

I tried to put the rejection behind me, write it off as a fluke, but it kept happening. Blonde, brunette's, short and tall women, hell even women older than me—they all said "no". That meant it was my fault right? What had I done to suddenly make women *not* want to jump into my bed?

I'd resorted to Googling *how to pick up women* like a pre-pubescent middle schooler.

Were my hands clammy when I shook her hand? Did I have something stuck in my teeth like broccoli or spinach? Or did my smile come across as creepy instead of sly and seductive?

Hollis walked over, pulling me back to the present, her hair was pulled into a high ponytail and her blonde curls cascaded down her shoulders. It had gotten a lot longer over the past few months, and it suited her. She smiled. "I know weddings are a great place to find single women who wished they were the bride, but it's hopeless tonight. I felt the need to tell you because seeing you looking around like a lost puppy dog was just sad."

I grinned and pulled her into a quick side hug. "Are you saying that because you secretly brought one of your single friends for me and you changed your mind at the last minute?"

"Please. If I had any single friends I wouldn't let them anywhere near you, and it's because my standards for your future girlfriend are incredibly high. None of them are good enough for you," she said, rubbing my side.

I let her go and narrowed my eyes. "I feel like you're just saying that. You know I don't do the whole commitment thing so why would it matter if someone was good enough for me?" I leaned down and lowered my voice to a whisper. "Or do they suck in bed, and you love me too much to let me experience that?"

Hollis gasped and smacked my chest. I rubbed the spot as Townes walked up behind her with a smile. "Hit him harder."

"Your wife is mean," I mumbled, earning me a shrug from Hollis.

We continued talking until the DJ came over the microphone and introduced Case and Basil back with their newly shared last name, *Whitlock*.

Everyone cheered as they rushed in, and when Case dipped her again in front of everyone, something tightened in my chest. I brushed off the feeling and rushed over to them when they were both back on their feet.

I pulled them both into a crushing hug. "Congrats you two."

"Thanks Scottie," Basil said, her smile never faltering even as she was pulled into Hollis's arms.

Townes came to my side and embraced Case. "You're a lucky man."

Case smiled at us both, and it was then I noticed his hand was still linked with Basil's. "Thanks guys, seriously. I don't know what I'd do without you both. Now if you'll excuse me, I need another moment with my wife before I have to share her attention with everyone else here."

We both nodded and watched him drag her to a secluded corner. My chest ached again when they were out of sight, and I decided the perfect way to get rid of it.

Beer.

Because if I couldn't find someone to keep me company tonight, then that was the next best thing.

I may have shoved some poor dude a little too hard out of the way earlier when we did the garter toss. But it was because I was under the impression that the little scrap of fabric was going to bring me luck in the dating field. I didn't know you had to already be in a committed relationship for the weird magic juju to work.

The guy's girlfriend glared at me as she held a napkin to his head, and I was too chicken shit to apologize. I felt bad, horrible even, but I was scared that if I got close enough she was going to cause some serious damage. So I made a B-line in the opposite direction and shoved the fabric into my pocket.

My counterpart on the ice, Riley, stepped to my side and patted my back. "You have a secret long-term girlfriend you haven't told me about Scottie?"

"If I had a girlfriend, it would be a sign the world was ending." I took my hand from my pocket and adjusted my tie. "Besides, dating is for people who are ready to settle down and that's not in the cards for me."

Me and dating didn't bode well together—the idea of commitment gave me hives and honestly it was a lot of work. I was so busy with my career in the NHL to even think about what it would be like to be in a relationship. I joined the Denver Peaks almost two years ago and was busy working on being the best left winger in the league. I already proved I was the best rookie during my first season with the team and now I needed to keep up that momentum.

Riley raised a brow. "You don't ever get lonely? I mean, almost everyone on the team is in a relationship and two of your closest friends are married."

The tightness in my chest shifted to the left and gripped my heart. I wasn't lonely, not in the way he was asking. Except for now.

Stupid dry spell.

Riley was a decent guy, he played opposite me as a right winger, and he was an awesome wingman whenever we went out together. But sometimes he said stuff that made me think too hard and it made me uncomfortable.

Like being lonely.

I stepped toward the bar. "Can't be lonely if you know you're not cut out for relationships." I walked away, taking the jab at myself with me.

It wasn't like I was lying. Aside from not having time for a relationship, I knew I wasn't cut out for them. Taking a woman on dates? Buying her gifts and doing small things for her? There were too many chances for me to fuck things up and it was easier to avoid that chance all together.

I was great at giving orgasms and walking away. That was it.

I reached the bar, ordered a beer, and sat on one of the few barstools available. They were the ones that spun too. *Score.* My eyes drifted over the crowd of dancing bodies, full of Case's family and our teammates. Then there was Basil's dad and stepmom, the only people she invited from her family. And like Hollis said, there were no single women lurking on the outskirts of the crowd waiting to be swept off their feet and away from the room.

I wasn't going to be anyone's knight in shining armor who made them forget how alone they were while my tongue was between their legs.

Jesus, I need to get laid.

Heels clicked on the wood floor behind me, but I

didn't turn around right away. It wasn't until she spoke with a smooth, lower register voice that I spun in the chair to look at her. God was she beautiful.

She wore a green satin dress, the material clung to her frame, leaving nothing to the imagination. Lean muscle hid under her skin, and I wondered if she was an athlete or if she was just dedicated to the gym. My attention caught on her long red hair that fell in loose curls down her back, covering the exposed skin where her dress dipped down to her hips.

The bartender placed her drink on the counter, a Tequila Sunrise, and she took it with a smile. She bit the straw and spun around to look at the crowd, either she was unaware I was burning a hole into the side of her pretty face or she was good at ignoring people.

I took a chance and reached out to tap her elbow. She faced me, and when her dark blue eyes met mine, my tongue turned to lead in my mouth. My gaze roamed over her freckled skin and square jaw before they caught onto the gold ring through her septum.

She raised a brow. "Can I help you?"

Shit, what was I supposed to say? *Hey you're the most stunning woman I've ever laid eyes on and I would love for you to crush me between your thighs?*

No. I was desperate, but I wasn't willing to mess this up.

I gave her my best smile and opened my mouth—but nothing came out except a groan of frustration. I laid my head on the counter and came to terms knowing my dry spell would last forever. My dick would never come out of hiding.

"Um, are you okay?" she asked.

I waved a hand, not picking my head up, and speaking

toward the ground. "Don't mind me. I seem to have forgotten how to talk to women and I can't subject you to this embarrassment." I sat up, my back ramrod straight as I tipped my head to her. "If you'll excuse me, I'm going to wallow in a corner."

A giggle escaped her, and I stopped mid step. I made her laugh. Did I still have it?

She blinked and a smile crossed her face. "Wallow? Why because you were stunned by my beauty?" she asked with a wink and a toss of her hair over her shoulder.

She was confident, and it was hot.

"That's actually exactly what happened." I chuckled and sat back down. "So would you please allow me to start over?"

"Sure. Just pretend I'm of average attractiveness, maybe that'll help?"

"Not at all, beautiful. You're the most stunning woman I've ever laid eyes on and you've ruined me for anyone else."

She let out a playful gasp and placed her hand on her chest. "Ruined you? That usually happens in the bedroom."

"I'll have you know that, between the sheets, I usually do the ruining sweetheart," I said, inching closer.

A smirk pulled on those red lips and she downed her drink before playing with the ends of her hair, as if she was teasing me by not giving me her undivided attention. "And I'll have you know I don't just let anyone ruin me. There are a few rules before I let a man try and live up to his promises."

"Oh? And what are they, if I may ask?" I leaned in closer and caught a whiff of coconut.

She walked her fingers over the counter until they

reached my hand, then she started drawing nonsense shapes over my skin. My entire body heated under her touch, but I kept my eyes on hers as she smiled.

"A single date that includes an activity, food, and a goodnight kiss."

Heat coated her words, and I dropped my head until we were eye level. "Does the night end with the kiss?"

"That's just one of the rules, I didn't say nothing else could happen outside of them."

I grinned. "Well why don't you finish your drink? I'd love to take you out."

"I think I'll take my time actually," she said, sticking her tongue out and gripping the straw with it.

This woman was going to kill me if she kept this up. I leaned back in the seat and spun back around, I looked over the crowd again and became curious.

"How do you know the bride and groom?" I asked. I hadn't seen her earlier when I was staring off into space, and Hollis didn't mention her. Unless she was one of those friends she was worried about not being good enough for me.

Not that that meant anything.

The woman cleared her throat and tapped her plastic cup. "I'm just a plus one tonight," she answered with a smile before giving me a once over. "How about you?"

I returned her smile, hearing her question but not really processing what she asked. "Do you really not know who I am?"

While I didn't expect her to know me, it would have been a little surprising considering she was a guest at a hockey player's wedding.

She shook her head. "Sorry, I'm not familiar with sports. I'm just here for the drinks."

Someone who didn't know who I was? Who was I to pass up on the chance of being anonymous for one night? I smiled. "I'm here for the drinks too, I'm a friend of the groom. What's your name? I don't think I caught it."

She finished her drink and held out her hand. "Clover, and before you tell me yours, I don't want to know. It's another rule. Can't get attached if I don't know who you are."

Her skin was warm, and I was obsessed with how small her hand was compared to mine. I smiled and started walking with her toward the doors. "That's actually really smart. You can call me whatever you want, I don't really have any name ideas. Unless you're into the daddy thing."

Clover shuddered and I had to keep from laughing.

"Absolutely not." A giggle escaped her. "Hm, I think we'll go with Hot Shot."

I opened the door and led her through in front of me. "I like it. But you're the only one who can call me that since it sounds so good coming from you. So don't go telling your friends."

She gave me another mocking gasp as the cold air hit us. "How dare you assume I'll tell anyone about you. If you're good enough in bed I'd want you to myself, but if you suck, I wouldn't subject you to the embarrassment of telling everyone I know. Don't worry, your secret nickname is safe with me," she said.

I caught another smile on her face and I wanted to kiss her.

But that would come later, after I fulfilled her little date rule. When we reached my car she was shivering, so I grabbed an extra blanket from the back and tucked her into the passenger seat before I got the heat going.

"So an activity first, or food?" I asked, pulling out of the lot. My mind tried to think of any restaurants I'd seen when I got into town.

Clover shook her head. "I'm not the one in charge here, you can make all the choices and find out later if they were the right ones."

I barked a laugh and my hand landed on her thigh before I could think better of it. "Alright alright, let's get some food then. Cause I don't know about you, but those little egg pies they had at the cocktail table weren't any good."

"Egg pies?" she asked, her brows furrowing. "Do you mean quiches?"

"Yeah those things." I gently squeezed her leg and glanced at her. "You okay with some fast food? I'm only asking cause while greasy food sounds great, I don't want you to ruin your pretty dress."

Clover smiled again and I had to keep myself from pulling her across the bench seat of the truck and into my side.

"Let me worry about the state of my dress, Hot Shot. Now, what kind of food did you have in mind?"

briar

Five years ago I vowed to never date another athlete unless they were willing to be a sugar daddy and I didn't have to be emotionally invested. But here I was, throwing my vow into the trash because I was too horny to care.

Tonight, the man in front of me wasn't Scottie Lancaster, left winger of the Denver Peaks. He was Hot Shot, and he kept staring at my boobs, not that I was doing anything to help the situation. In fact, I was doing the opposite by leaning over the table to talk to him with a flirtatious smile and my hand on his wrist.

I couldn't help it. He was hot, with his red curls and dark blue eyes. This was my last night of freedom before I had a new roommate who would report back to my dad if I stepped out of line.

Okay, I was being dramatic, but that's what it felt like.

I was going to enjoy my time tonight before I kissed celibacy on the cheek and closed my legs for the year. Scottie took me to a sleazy diner where everyone looked either hungover or ready to commit arson after they loaded up on food so greasy I could use it to fix something on a car. What exactly, I didn't know—I wasn't a mechanic. I was a girl who wrote articles highlighting women in male dominated fields. Mayors, women in stems, and my favorite—sports. My blog didn't make headlines, but it had a decent following. Women all over the world liked to send emails about how my words motivated them to pursue degrees in engineering, finance, and all the other things society told them was a man's job.

While I didn't attend the ceremony—I had to acclimate to the change in altitude—I made sure to attend the reception where I could stuff my face with tiny food and free alcohol. The captain of the hockey team my dad coached was the one who had gotten hitched, and while I had only met Case Whitlock once or twice, I had no desire to get to know anyone else on the team. All the hockey players I'd met were all the same—self-absorbed, egotistical assholes who didn't care about stomping on your feelings.

I'd seen pictures and heard stories of Scottie. How he played the field at parties and never turned a woman down who came onto him. He was no different than the rest of them, but he was cute enough that I wasn't going to turn him down. If I was being honest, I saw the appeal and I really needed to get laid.

"So tell me something," he said, picking at the limp fries on his plate. "How come I didn't see you at the wedding? I know you're short, but I had a decent vantage point as a groomsman, and you weren't there."

I sipped on my lemonade and caught the way his eyes darted to my neck as I swallowed. His dark blue eyes had a look to them that said he wasn't afraid to beg, and it made my skin heat.

"Here's the thing." I set the cup down. "Wedding ceremonies give me hives. Everyone around you is either happy for the couple, resentful of their own relationship and radiate jealousy, or are single and hoping to find their happily ever after. So I showed up at the reception, where everyone started drinking enough to forget about their own problems and have fun. Also, I got sick from the altitude, so I was chugging water and taking Aspirin like it was my job."

Hot Shot blinked. His expression went blank before he cleared his throat and reached for his drink. "How many weddings did it take before you realized you were allergic to happiness?"

I smirked. "Three, and all of them were my mom's."

"Your parents aren't together?" he asked.

We were treading into territory that was off limits to anyone who wasn't in my top five emergency contacts list, so it was time for a change in subject.

I batted my lashes. "Where are you taking me when we're done here, Hot Shot?"

He stuck his tongue in his cheek and heat rushed up my spine. "You got a curfew, Clover?"

"Nope. I'm simply thinking about how much longer until you rip off this dress if things keep going as well as they are."

Scottie stood from his seat, reached into his pocket, and tossed a few twenties down on the table before he reached for my hand. He tugged me out of the booth and gave the waitress a wave as we left the diner. The winter air stung my cheeks as we walked out, and he pulled me into his side in an attempt to keep me warm. Lemon and linen welcomed me, and it was hard not to rub my face into his chest.

He smelled fantastic, sue me.

He opened the door to his truck and wrapped the green down blanket around me before he went around and put the keys in the ignition. We started down the road before the car heated all the way, and I could still see his breath when he breathed out.

"Aren't you cold? Do you want the blanket?"

"Sure," he said.

Before I could adjust the fabric so it was long enough to cover him, he reached across the bench seat and placed his hand on my outer thigh. Then he pulled me toward him, I was right up against him in a heartbeat. He grinned and covered his legs with the blanket before he threw his arm over my shoulders and placed a kiss on the top of my head.

I was grateful he was focused on the road, otherwise he would have seen that my flabbers were gasted. My jaw went slack, and I had to keep a giggle from announcing itself. His fingers traced up and down my arm as he drove.

"Where are you taking me?" I asked.

He turned left and started going up the small hill. "You'll see soon enough."

I remained quiet as we continued down the road until eventually a parking lot came into view. There were no cars and everything was covered in a soft blanket of snow. It was untouched and I almost felt bad when Hot Shot made a parking spot for himself. He looked down at me with furrowed brows. "I should have thought this through."

"Thought what through?" I asked.

He was quiet for a moment, glancing out to the snow before offering me a soft smile. "You're going to have to keep the blanket wrapped around you okay? But if you get too cold, can you promise to let me know?"

"Of course," I said.

Hot Shot gave me a curt nod before he shut off the ignition. He rounded the car, having no issues walking through the two feet of snow with those long legs of his. The door opened and snow whipped around me, causing me to hold the blanket tighter to my body. He placed careful hands over my shoulder and lower back to help ease me out of the car before he moved behind me and settled those same hands on my hips. The blanket was thick, but I swore his hands were burning themselves through the layers of fabric to my skin.

The rules thing was something I pulled out of my butt —I didn't have a set of requirements someone had to meet before I slept with them. I simply told him that because he was cute and I selfishly wanted to see how seriously he'd take them, considering his reputation.

His hands tightened a bit when I slipped on a patch of ice, and his breath brushed against my cold ear when he spoke, a smile playing on his lips. "Careful Clover. Can't let you get hurt before I show you why I brought you all the way up here."

We walked a few feet further, a short brick wall was arranged in a semicircle around us and the trees beyond it were bare with only snow covering the thin branches. With soft, steady steps, Hot Shot led me to the edge of the wall. Below was a snow covered, rocky ledge that promised a few broken bones if anyone fell down it. Beyond that though, when I lifted my eyes, were lights.

Most of them were where downtown Breckinridge sat, with a few more scattered elsewhere. The warm light reflected off the snow, covering the area below in a soft, almost warm glow. The wind picked up and I watched it carry snow into the sky, flurries danced in the empty space. My cheeks burned as I turned to give the handsome man behind me a smile. His focus though was on what laid beyond us, and that was fine. It gave me time to trace over his features—so masculine, yet they held an edge of boyish softness to them. His jaw was solid, but not harsh, his nose was straight, yet it upturned a little at the very end. Not something anyone would notice right away, but I picked it out easily enough with our proximity.

Then there were the soft barely there curls in his red hair, like he styled them away just for tonight. The red in his hair was similar to mine, though mine was a shade lighter.

The pressure around my hips disappeared and I whirled around to find Hot Shot on his phone. Before I could question what he was doing, music started playing. He placed the phone back into his pocket and held out a hand, his fingertips red from the cold.

I rushed toward him and grabbed them, rubbing furiously to warm them up. "Are you kidding? You have a damn blanket in your car but no gloves?"

His hands were huge in mine. I tried my best not to focus on the veins running over the tops of them—because let's be real, veiny hands were my kryptonite—and sandwiched the tips of his fingers between my hands before blowing into the space. They were still frosty when I inspected them again.

I looked up at the irresponsible man, ready to demand we go back to the car, but froze when I saw the gleam in those dark blue eyes.

"What?"

"Dance with me," he said.

My mouth opened on a protest, but he was too fast. His hands slipped beneath the blanket and settled over my dress, an inch below where my skin was exposed. I fought a shiver when he touched me again, but I wasn't sure if it was from how cold they were or something else.

Shit. I was falling—hard. This wasn't supposed to happen. All I'd wanted to do tonight was see if that thing I saw on my social media feed was true. That Scottie was a heartbreaker with no concern for anyone but himself. The Scottie who stood in front of me was the complete opposite of what people were saying about him online.

"Dance with me," he said again, tugging my body until we were chest to chest. "You can keep me warm now." He leaned closer and nipped the top of my ear. "And I'll keep you warm later."

I swooned so hard that if he wasn't holding onto me, I would have collapsed in the snow. But the flush covering my body would have been enough to keep me warm as I laid there.

Everything was fine.

I let him lead me in small circles, my sheer tights were soaked and my toes were numb, but I was having too much fun to care.

It wasn't until my teeth were clattering together that Hot Shot took me back to the car, and like the times before, he helped me in first and bundled the blanket around me tighter. When he turned the car on, he pulled me into his side again and rubbed my arm. He leaned his head on mine. "Was that a good enough activity?"

I didn't have the energy to find words, so I nodded.

"You're cold." He pulled away and at the same time pushed me to sit straight so my eyes were on his. "You promised you'd let me know when you got cold."

For half a second, I let myself pull those words apart. It was clear where this night was leading but the sincerity in his voice was jarring. His words carried the soft concern you'd hear from a long-term lover, not some random hookup, and I had to stop myself from peeling the words apart and finding something that wasn't there.

We'd never see each other again once our time together was done and I hated to admit to myself how much that sucked.

My hand landed on his thigh before my fingers slowly dragged up his leg. He sucked in a breath, the look in his eyes shifting from concern to something heated.

"So am I going to get that goodnight kiss here or somewhere more comfortable?"

Hot Shot sucked in a breath through his nose and bit the inside of his cheek before he started out of the parking lot. "Where are you staying? You can plug it into the GPS, the code to my phone is two, four—"

"Not my hotel," I spit out. He raised a brow. "I uh—am sharing a room with someone and that would be rude to bring someone by."

I wasn't sharing a room with anyone, but my dad was staying in the next room over and the hotel walls were thin.

It didn't get past me how he gripped the steering wheel tighter. "So what do you want to do then?"

"What do you mean?" I asked.

"I mean, if we can't go back to your place then what are you comfortable doing? I can give you that goodnight kiss on the side of the road, in front of your hotel, or I can take you to where I'm staying. I've got the place to myself."

It was cute he was asking, as if he didn't know that the last option was the only one worth picking. I tapped his inner thigh. "Your place sounds nice."

It sounded like he said "thank fuck" but he was speaking too low for me to be certain.

The drive to where he was staying was quick despite the snow-covered roads, though he did take extra care when he turned into a long driveway. When we reached the front door, he stared down at me, his hands on my hips to keep me steady because while the top half of my body was fine, my legs and toes were still cold.

I stared up at him and smiled. "I had fun tonight."

"Yeah? I'm glad."

"Mhm, the food was great, and the activity was super fun. I've never been to a scenic overlook before."

His brows rose as a boyish grin crossed his face. "Really? I like going whenever I need to think about stuff. There's one near Denver I go to a lot."

"What kind of stuff?" I asked, and wished I hadn't. Scottie and I didn't need to know anything about each other. We'd share this night together and I'd spend the year avoiding him, never going to games or practices. Besides, he wouldn't remember me anyway. I cleared my throat and stepped closer into his chest, his heart beating against mine. "You don't have to answer that by the way— I'm stalling."

He brushed a strand of hair behind my ear. "Why?"

"Cause I really want you to kiss me, but what if you're bad at it."

Strong fingers wrapped around the back of my neck, two of them threaded through my hair as Hot Shot pulled close enough that I could taste the faint peppermint on his breath. "I've been told I'm *very* good at kissing, but maybe it's something you'll have to test for yourself."

"Yes please."

Lips pressed against mine and I let my legs turn to

jelly, which was fine because Hot Shot was still supporting me. The blanket fell to my feet and with one hand on my hip, pulling me against him, and one in my hair—I turned into a mess. *We* were a mess as his tongue brushed against my lower lip and he let out a groan. He spun me around and somehow managed to unlock the door. My head was dizzy as he walked me backward, my heels hit the wood floors for a second before I was being lifted and wrapping my legs around his waist where I found him hard and eager as his hips rolled into mine.

I was vaguely aware of us moving somewhere, Hot Shot kept his hands firmly on my ass as he walked us to our destination, and I spent my time kissing his neck so he didn't walk us into a wall. A door opened and I was being thrown onto a bed with plush blankets, Hot Shot crawled over me, shoving his knee between my legs to spread them apart.

I grinned and shimmied under him, searching for his touch. He smirked before kissing me again, he gripped both of my wrists in one hand and moved them above my head before moving down my neck.

"Is this that *ruining* you were talking about?" I asked.

He looked at me through those dark lashes, heat pouring out of his eyes so hot it rivaled what was going on in my body.

"Oh sweetheart, I'm just getting started."

briar

I wish he knew my name.

I told myself that if I went to that wedding and happened to leave with anyone, I was going to keep my identity a secret. No one needed to know my birthday, how old I was, or my name. But when Hot Shot's hand caressed my inner thigh again, I wished I had told him so I could hear it leave his lips. He was more than attractive—I felt like I needed to call Forbes and get him on some kind of list for hot people—and I was surprised when he dropped that horrible pickup line earlier. Not because he was out of my league or anything, but I had expected women to be fawning over him all night.

How could they not? His shoulders were broad under his well fitted button up, his curly red hair brushed above his brows, and his smile was electrifying. Then there were his hands, large and calloused with veins big enough they were perfect if he ever decided to be a hand model.

Shit was I drooling over *hands?*

He pushed my legs open more with his free hand and leaned in, his nose brushing my temple as his fingers drifted into dangerous territory. Soft, barely there touches caressed over my skin and sent heat up to my chest as I heaved in a breath.

"You're mighty red Clover." His nose brushed down to my jaw and I felt his breath on my exposed neck. "How wet will I find you if I touch you here?" he asked, his fingers a whisper away from the seam of my thong.

"Why don't you touch me and find out?" I arched into his touch, but he pulled away.

I shook my head and took a shaky breath, heat burning through my body as I tugged where he held my wrists captive. This wasn't fair. He had those blue *please give it to me* eyes, yet there I was, getting ready to beg him.

His finger hooked around my underwear at the same time he ran his tongue along my jaw. "You know, I've been following your little *rules* all night. I fed you, took you to a beautiful overlook, and even kissed you goodnight."

"What's your point?" I asked, my nipples hardening the more he teased me.

I could feel him smile against my throat, then gasped when his finger grazed my clit.

"My point is, now it's time you follow *my rules.*"

My brain was mush. I couldn't breathe when he was so close to where I wanted him. He pulled away and a whine escaped me.

His hand was in my hair, fingers gripping the nape of my neck. "Look at me pretty girl."

I did.

"Good," he said. "Rules are simple. You come when I say you can."

It wasn't fair, but I was at his mercy and there wasn't a better place to be. I nodded and then met his lips again as he started working me out of my dress. There was a tear, but I didn't care enough about the dress to say anything. My focus was on Hot Shot and how he worked swiftly to get me naked with only one hand.

If there was an Olympic sport for it, he'd win gold.

I wasn't wearing a bra, so when he finally tore away the fabric, my nipples pebbled against the cool air. He sucked in a breath and wasted no time enveloping one in his mouth, leaving the other to wait in agony. He still hadn't let my hands go and I didn't think he was going to anytime soon.

My hips bucked against him, seeking out some sort of friction to ease the ache between my legs.

He pulled back and smirked. "Someone's impatient," I whined into my shoulder, and he chuckled before gripping my chin and forcing me to face him. "Tell me what you need."

"I need to you fuck me."

He dropped his mouth to mine and ground against me, I felt every inch of him, and I was almost embarrassed of the whine that escaped me. He readjusted himself so he was caging my legs between his, forcing me to stay still as he continued to kiss my hot skin and play with my nipples with calloused fingers. There was no way to keep track of how many times his mouth met my skin, sucking at the sensitive neck of my collarbone. I was too lost in the feeling to care. It wasn't until he let out a low growl and pulled away that I realized he was struggling with something.

"Fuck, I—" He shook his head. "I usually have more control than this, but I think I need to fuck you too."

His grip around my wrists slackened and I went for his clothes. He released my legs but kept his thighs planted on either side of my hips. I unbuttoned his shirt and then his belt without a care where anything landed. I gave his slacks a good tug before he forced me down onto my back as he braced me between his muscular arms. I shoved a hand into the front of them and gave him a long stroke through his boxers.

He shuddered against me and a rough gasp escaped him before he pulled away. His eyes stayed on mine as he removed his remaining clothes and my skin burned as I took in his body. The defined muscles on his shoulders and chest, the abs, and the happy trail that went down…

He was *huge.*

The heat in my stomach turned to nerves as he kissed me again, interlocking his fingers with mine as he stroked himself. I was tense under him when I felt him lay heavy on my thigh, and he pulled away, leaving a gentle kiss on my collarbone.

"You okay?"

God he was a gentleman.

I nodded, pushing my nerves to the side. "I'm okay, just nervous."

"Why?" he asked, moving farther in the opposite direction.

I giggled as I wove my fingers through his hair. "Because I'm scared you'll split me in two, and I want to enjoy this."

Hot Shot laughed and the sound hit me square in the chest. "I think I can help with that."

He kissed my nose and kissed down my body until he was between my legs, looking back at me with a question in his eyes. There was something about the constant checking in that made my heart soar. I nodded and watched as his lids closed before he put two fingers in his mouth. My heart rate kicked up at the sight, then as soon as those fingers touched me, I soared. My hips bucked and my hands went to grab his hair as he worked me.

He continued to place gentle kisses over me as if he wasn't destroying me with his touch. Then when he assumed that was enough, he removed those fingers and held my eyes as he put them back in his mouth.

This man was so dirty.

When he pulled away, he reached into the side table drawer and pulled out a square foil packet. I bit my lip as I watched him slide on the condom. Then he got back onto the bed and placed a kiss on my collar bone as he aligned himself. He caught my mouth with his as he entered me in one motion. I'd have gasped if I'd been able to breathe. The intrusion was a wonderful sensation, and it only took me a moment before I nodded, encouraging him to continue. My nails carved themselves into his back as he pulled out slowly, begging for *something*.

That something was the powerful thrust of his hips back into me, making colors dance across my eyes. He placed his hand on my neck as he fucked the memory of my own name out of me. I was forced to look at him as he made a mess of me, my eyes darting between the heat in his eyes and the way his chest heaved with every thrust.

At some point he released me and bent my legs to my chest. Then he got onto the bed and started fucking *down* into me. My orgasm crashed into me like a freight train. I gripped his arms, not knowing if I wanted to push him away or pull him toward me.

He groaned and thrust into me two more times before a shiver wracked through his whole body. I lay there in a mess as he placed kisses over my body which I found odd. I'd had one-night stands enough times to know this wasn't a common thing, but still, I couldn't find it in myself to pull away from him. I watched as he removed the condom and threw it in a small trash bin next to the side table it came from.

Hot Shot got into the bed next to me and dragged a finger up my leg. "The bathroom is right there." He gestured to the door in the right corner of the room. "I'll go get drinks while you get cleaned up."

He placed a kiss on my cheek, grabbed his boxers from the mess of clothes on the floor, and left the room. I half considered leaving, it was standard procedure after a quick hookup. But also, casual aftercare and I weren't friends, it screamed intimacy and that was at the bottom of the list of things I was looking for.

At the top of that list? A good chemical free tampon so I didn't have to worry about toxic shock syndrome.

Nerves ate away at my skin as I picked up my dress, neatly folded it, and placed it on the bench at the foot of the bed. I laid back in the bed, thong back on, and stared at the ceiling as I contemplated the repercussions of my decision—the main one being my dad would likely implode if he ever found out what we did.

I was lost in thought and didn't notice when Hot Shot reentered the room, a glass of water in one hand and a small plate of cookies in the other. My stomach grumbled at the sight and I shoved a pillow over it to smother the noise.

His brows pulled together before he set the things down and grabbed a shirt from the dresser. He tossed it at me before smiling. "A post orgasm cookie is always a good choice," he said as he held out the plate.

I put the shirt on and took a cookie without question, refusing the water. "Was this something you came up with?"

"Nah. I had a one-night stand in Toronto a year ago and she's the one that put me onto it."

The cookie had the perfect consistency, and I laid back into the sheets. "Bold of you to talk about your past one-night stands when your current one is still next to you."

Hot Shot leaned down and placed a casual kiss on the top of my head before grabbing another cookie. "Considering we don't know each other's names, I figured you wouldn't care. But if you secretly do, then we can pretend this conversation never happened and I found this recipe on Pinterest."

I raised a brow. "You have Pinterest?"

"Yes. But only because my sisters like to add me as a collaborator on their stuff so I know what gifts to buy them for the holidays."

The honesty caught me off guard, but I couldn't do anything except finish off the cookie and reach for the water. Hot Shot rolled onto his back and sighed. "So tell me something Clover, what's with all the mystery and rules?"

"Do you actually want an answer or are you buying time so you can jump my bones again in a few minutes?" I asked with a teasing smile.

Hot Shot placed a hand over his chest. "You've wounded me, I'd never buy time with small talk." He opened his eyes and leaned in close to my ear. "I'd buy it with my tongue between your legs."

My cheeks heated but I couldn't pull my eyes away from his, he was teasing me, and he was getting the reaction he wanted. I liked to think I was a strong woman, but when a handsome man said dirty things I turned into who I was when I first discovered fan fiction.

So I focused on his question and figured that since

we'd never see each other again, the truth wouldn't hurt. I cleared my throat and rubbed my fingers along the satin sheets. "I don't like the idea of people searching for me online after we've parted ways, and the date is so I know I'm not sleeping with assholes. They don't buy you food and tend to press when you bring up protection." I shrugged. "So I'm just protecting myself."

He was quiet for a long moment before he placed his hand on my leg and squeezed. "I'm sorry you've had to deal with that, that's not fair to you."

I reached for another cookie and broke it in half. "I've learned to live with it, you don't need to feel sorry for me. And if it's any consolation"—I peered up at him, and for the first time tonight was honest with him—"I'd give you my real name cause you brought me cookies and were a very respectable gentleman."

He grinned, and the sight made my chest tight with an emotion I couldn't place. I shook my head, hoping the feeling would go away.

"Well I hate to burst your little bubble Clover girl, but I like not knowing your name. It means I can't go after you and ruin my bachelor lifestyle."

I nodded. "So that's what all this is? I'm just another notch in your bed post?"

His brows furrowed. "Are you upset? If so, I can make you into a car freshener or something, it'd be vanilla and coconut scented."

"No there's no need for that, if anything that'll make you miss me and I'm not interested in being anyone's booty call."

"That's a shame, because I was just about to ask that," he said with a cocky smile on his face.

I finished my cookie and pulled the sheet further up

my chest, for no other reason than because Hot Shot kept staring and I wanted to be a tease. "So this bachelor lifestyle, tell me all about it."

He moved to lay down and his eyes shut when his head hit the pillow. "Mm I think I'd rather get some sleep, it's been a busy day. What do you like to eat in the mornings? I make amazing pancakes."

I reached for another cookie and batted my lashes. "Bold of you to assume I'll be staying the night."

His hand shot up and gently wrapped around my wrist, those blue eyes held me hostage as his thumb traced my skin. "If you don't want to, that's fine. I can take you back to your hotel, give you a goodnight kiss under some horrible lighting, and we'll go our separate ways. But Clover girl…" He leaned in and placed a kiss on my collarbone. "I'd really like it if you stayed the night. I'm an excellent cuddler."

I shook my head, at war with myself because staying was the worst thing I could do. What if I let it slip that I knew who he was? Or worse, what if he realized who *I* was? The only thing delaying my answer was the promise of cuddles—I haven't had those since college, and my body was tired, my eyes were heavy with sleep, and going back to that lumpy queen-sized mattress sounded horrible.

I pulled my hand away and finished off my cookie before lifting the sheets and getting myself comfortable. "You better be a man of your word. Otherwise, I'll make sure every single woman in the city knows you can't cuddle and that your breath smells like tuna."

His face dropped. "No it doesn't. Right? Holy shit, if I spent all night with tuna breath I'll—"

"Your breath smells fine, I was just making a funny," I

said before turning my head into the pillow. "Maybe I should leave since you think I'm insulting you."

He chuckled and placed a kiss on my shoulder. "Insult me all you want. I'll be too busy looking at you to care what you say."

I smiled to myself, closed my eyes, and prepared for a night of cuddles.

scottie

The smell of coconut coaxed me out of sleep and I blinked against the light beaming in, making a mental note to finally buy those blackout curtains that'd been sitting in my shopping cart. My arm tightened around my overnight guest and my fingers brushed the exposed skin of her hips where her shirt was bunched. I enjoyed the feel of goosebumps under my fingertips. I pushed my nose into her hair and took in a deep breath, which was weird—usually when I woke up next to a woman in my bed I had no urge to cuddle. That was reserved for the middle of the night because when I closed my eyes my body temperature liked to plummet, cuddling was my only chance of survival.

Otherwise, I had a routine; get up, make a *thanks for the sex* breakfast, then give an excuse of being late for practice with the promise to call later when I was done. Sometimes I did call if my sleepover buddy was chill and didn't go overboard with the fangirling.

Clover though, she was different, but I couldn't put my finger on why. Maybe her red hair, long legs, and freckles decorating her body had me under a spell. It didn't matter though, considering I had my own rules when it came to one-night stands.

No feelings.

No morning physical affection.

And no one stayed after breakfast. Period.

It was easier to put up unbreakable walls than rebuild them with a broken heart. The idea of giving myself to someone, wholly as I was, and being destroyed when I wasn't wanted anymore, scared me more than contracting an STD. That shit I could prevent with condoms and fix with antibiotics.

I was already breaking one rule and needed to get my shit together, if anything I needed to be celebrating. Clover had cured me of my dry spell—I should thank her.

She stirred slightly as I lowered my nose to her jawline and started pressing light kisses over her soft skin. My hand untangled itself from her waist and started traveling up her stomach. I was getting ready to pinch her already perk nipple when she arched her back, her ass pressing into my hardening cock. I groaned into her neck as I cupped her breast and rocked my hips into her.

"Good morning," I said as I peppered kisses down her neck.

She wiggled out of my hold and batted her lashes up at me, a sleepy smile on her face. "Morning Hot Shot, sleep well?"

"I did. How about you?"

Her gaze dropped to my naked chest and she placed her index finger in the middle of it. "Oh pretty good, had a really good dream too."

A shiver ran through me. "Is that so? Want to tell me about it?"

She shook her head and dragged her hand down to my boxers, running her finger over the hard ridges of my cock.

"I'd rather show you," she said as she lowered herself under the sheets.

I kept one hand on her head as she disappeared, the next thing I knew she was pulling off my boxers then— nothing. There was a moment I considered reassuring her that she didn't have to do anything she didn't want to, that I was perfectly fine if she decided not to—

In one swift motion she took all of me and I hit the back of her throat. I had to keep from bucking my hips up too much for fear of unintentionally hurting her. She gagged around me before moving up, all I heard was one gasp before she went down again. My hand twisted around her hair, but I didn't force her movements. If anything, it was to anchor me to reality so I didn't go crazy as she sucked my dick.

I wasn't a huge fan of blow jobs if I was being honest, and it was because most women I slept with were more concerned about themselves. Not that I was complaining, I was a munch through and through, but if I did get a blow job it wasn't great. So I never expected them and took whatever I got for the most part.

Clover though—I'd get on my knees, beg for her real name, and kiss her feet if that was what it took to get her to do this again.

Heat pooled in my stomach. I was going to come soon.

"Fuck—I—wher—"

She picked up speed and I felt my body tighten, my hand tugged on her hair, a silent warning to move that she didn't take. I let out a groan as my hips bucked and I spilled into her mouth. As I laid back to catch my breath, completely spent, she peeked back out from the sheets. A smug smile on her face.

"Good?"

I huffed out a laugh. "You give me a blow job first thing in the morning, and you ask if it was good? Yes." I reached out and moved a strand of hair out of her face. "It was good more than that actually. I might have to steal you because I want more of those."

She laughed. "Well hate to burst your bubble, but that was a onetime thing."

I reached for her, ready to return the favor when my phone rang from the bedside table. I could have ignored it, but I'd assigned different ringtones to my contacts and Coach's was currently playing.

Rolling over with the intention of cutting the call short, I placed my free hand on Clover's leg and answered the phone.

"Morning boss, to what do I owe the pleasure of your stoic, fatherly sounding voice," I said.

Coach Warner sighed on the other line, but I knew he was smiling. He always enjoyed my antics. "I'm calling to make sure you haven't forgotten about our meeting when we get back to town?"

I didn't. Coach and I were supposed to meet up so I could meet his daughter the day after tomorrow, he'd been hounding me all month how important this meeting was—so I decided to fuck with him.

"Shit,' I said, throwing Clover a wink when she gave me a furrowed expression. I planted a kiss on her forehead and smiled. "I think I've actually got something that day, can we reschedule?"'

"Are you serious," he asked in a deadpan voice. I could

practically see the vein in his forehead pulsating so I kept my laughter to myself.

I shook my head. "Of course not Coach, I'll see you when we get back to town."

The only answer I got was the click of the phone, I had thoroughly pissed him off, but it was all in good fun. He rarely took me seriously, and I think he was always upset with himself for falling for my poor jokes time and time again. I set the phone back on the nightstand when Clover rolled over, her hair fell over her shoulder and sleep filled her eyes. She was squinting up at me and made no move to get up.

"How long before I need to do the walk of shame?"

I chuckled and leaned in to place a kiss on her shoulder. "Take your time, Clover. I'm going to make us some breakfast, then take you back to your hotel, unless you want to stay longer. It's up to you."

She sat up and stretched her lean arms over her head, and you bet your ass I took the chance to take in every inch of her. "What kind of breakfast?" she asked, her eyes still squinted.

"Are your eyes okay? Do you need drops or anything?"

She shook her head. "I took out my contacts in the middle of the night and kind of can't see much of anything. I'll be fine though, promise."

We stared at each other for a long moment, I took in her soft features as she took in mine—well I assumed she was taking in my handsomeness and was plotting how she was going to get my number so we could do this again. Which we wouldn't because of those damn rules, and as much as I'd be willing to make an exception—I couldn't.

I had a reputation to uphold and needed to start planning my next night out with the guys.

I smiled and pulled my hand away, getting out of bed. I grabbed a fresh pair of sweats before turning toward her. "Hope you like chocolate chip pancakes. I make them all the time for my niece and she demolishes them. And once your belly is full, we'll go from there."

After I checked into the Airbnb I went straight to the grocery store for essentials. Which was; ingredients for pancakes, orange juice, and some microwavable dinners. While that last item might send my nutritionist into a panic, I figured one time wouldn't hurt.

Clover got out of the bed, a bit sluggish, and I had to make an effort to keep my eyes above her waist. It was difficult, but I was a gentleman after all. She squinted around the bed before meeting my gaze, her cheeks tinged pink. "You mind? I need to change."

"What's wrong with what you're wearing?"

"I'm naked?" she said.

I raised a brow. "And?"

"Oh my gosh, go cook before I sneak out the window," she said through a laugh.

I nodded and threw her a wink as my hand gripped the doorknob. "See you downstairs in a few."

As she changed, I got our food ready—bacon, eggs, and chocolate chip pancakes. A well-rounded meal to get the day started. After I took the last pancake out of the pan the doorbell rang. I quickly walked down the empty hall, this Airbnb was a total steal and seemed like the better option between it and a hotel. I even offered Townes and Riley to stay so we could all share the cost, but they both refused. Townes insisted if he stayed with me then Hollis would divert her attention to me—not true unless we were playing card games and she was accusing me of cheating—and Riley claimed he already had a place to stay.

So imagine my surprise when I opened the door and found Townes standing there with Hollis at his side, a grin on her face.

"Good morning!" she said as she walked in to give me a hug. Townes was right behind her and all I got from him was a nod—one day I'd get a hug, some way or another I'd finally crack his hard exterior and aversion to platonic physical affection.

"Hey," he said, stepping over the threshold and shutting the door. "She wanted to stop by and see you before we headed home."

Hollis pulled away and winked. "Townes also wanted to check on you since we didn't see you last night."

Townes mumbled something under his breath and headed toward the kitchen, and I followed right behind him with a grin. "Ah you're checking up on me? I'm flattered dude, I always knew you had a soft spot for me."

He stopped in front of a plate of chocolate chip pancakes, staring at them for a second before grabbing one and grumbling again. Hollis laughed and grabbed a plate before grabbing a few for herself. It was a good thing I always made more than necessary.

"So where is she? Still upstairs?" Hollis asked.

I nodded. "Yes, so if you guys wouldn't mind eating on the road? I've got plans for when she comes downstairs."

Townes whipped his head around with a scowl. "Don't be gross. We don't need to know every detail of your sex life."

"Calm down, that wasn't what I was talking about." I crossed my arms and leaned against the countertop. "For once."

When I was cooking breakfast, I had an insane idea to take Clover on a little *date.* Nothing serious, but I didn't want to part from her so soon. I looked up a few shops in town that I wanted to take her to. For just today I wanted to stay in the little bubble we created and get to know her a little more. Maybe even convince her that being a booty call wouldn't be the worst thing in the world if it meant we got to see each other again.

"That smells good."

Townes, Hollis, and I turned toward that sweet, silky, sleep-filled voice. My breath hitched a little when I saw Briar standing in the middle of the stairs. She wore that silk dress from last night and her hair was braided over her shoulder. Her cheeks were a bright shade of red as her narrowed eyes darted between me and our company.

"Hi! Sorry to be a bother but we were simply here for the food. We'll be out of your hair in just a second," Hollis said as she shoved pancakes into her mouth. I waited for Townes to say something, make a noncommittal grunt, or tell me how much I fucked up because Clover was way out of my league. Instead, he just looked at her, his scowl deepening.

Clover waved a hand. "Oh no worries, I was actually heading out."

"What?" I asked, rounding the island to reach her at the bottom of the stairs. I followed her as she made her way to the door. "You're not staying?"

She shook her head. "Can't. I've got places to be. Thanks though. For"—her cheeks reddened as she looked at the floor—"last night. I had a lot of fun."

I wanted to reach out to stop her, beg her to stay so we could spend the day together like I'd imagined. But I also knew I couldn't stop her, so I asked the only question I could think of. "Can I at least get your number?"

"I don't think that's a good idea."

"Oh," I said.

A horn honked outside, and Clover shook her head. "Bye Hot Shot."

God I wanted to kiss her, but held myself back because I knew if I did, she wouldn't be leaving. I'd take her back upstairs and beg her to stay. So instead, I smiled and reached out to touch the back of her hand with my fingertips. "Bye Clover. Stay safe getting home."

When I walked back into the kitchen, I was met with something I thought I'd never seen before. Townes was smiling. Not at me or Hollis, but down at his phone as he typed something furiously. I approached him slowly—afraid something was wrong with him—while Hollis continued eating her pancakes like nothing strange was happening at her side.

"You okay?" I asked.

Townes, still smiling, shook his head and looked up at me. He put his phone in his pocket and threw a tattooed arm over Hollis's shoulders.

"Everything's fine," he said.

I wasn't going to poke the bear and demand answers. I grabbed food and took the seat across from Hollis, trying to keep my thoughts from wandering to Clover and dwelling on the fact I'd never see her again.

briar

"Dad I don't need you to chaperone this, seriously just drop me off at the house and I'll meet him after the game tonight," I said as I followed dad into a local diner.

Holding the door open, he clicked his tongue and shook his head. "I've already told you how important it was to me that I facilitate this meeting between the two of you. Besides, there are some important things I need to discuss with the both of you."

We followed the hostess to our booth, and I opened the menu. "Like what?" I asked.

"I'll tell you both when he gets here," he said.

The only thing I knew about my new roommate was he played on the Peaks. Dad failed to mention anything else about him and no amount of pleading got him to fork over the information. After combing through the updated roster I found online, I knew I had about five options to pick from—six if he was including Scottie in his choices.

I wasn't hungry, and was planning on leaving the second I said hello to whoever dad picked to be my roommate. There was no need to exchange pleasantries with someone I had no intention of ever interacting with outside of a run-in over breakfast.

"But before he *does* get here, we need to have a serious talk about expectations," Dad said with a raised brow. His blond hair had more grey in it than it used to and his glasses were thicker.

Expectations? Oh.

I covered my ears. "Can we not have this conversation in the middle of a family restaurant?"

"It's a much-needed discussion if you're going to—"

"La la la la la," I said as he continued rambling. We'd had the very awkward sex talk when I went through puberty, and every year since then, but it was hard to fault him for being protective. I was his only child after all. He wanted the best for me but that didn't mean I was going to subject myself to this. I went to move out of the booth, an excuse on my lips about using the bathroom, but a giant gift basket stopped me.

My gaze traveled upward and red hair caught my attention, then dark blue eyes that stared into my soul as I crumpled under them.

Hot Shot. Scottie.

Holy fuck. Fucking fucking shit balls.

He had a gift basket. Was it a ploy to woo some sweet, innocent woman into his bed and, wait—was that a stuffed *panda* in that thing? I wanted it.

No. Why is he here?

Dad grinned and waved his hand as an invitation for Hot Shot to join us. "You made it! Hope traffic wasn't terrible."

Scottie's eyes were still on me as he smiled and held out a hand toward the booth. "May I?"

"Briar, move over for the man," Dad said.

He handed me the gift basket, and I placed it against the wall, trying not to look at the panda as our server walked up and took our drink orders. I decided on a strawberry margarita and tried to get an extra shot, but Dad said it was too early to start day drinking. So I supposed I was going to be relatively sober while I sat next to the man who made me see stars.

Great.

"Hon this is Scottie, he's the one you're going to be rooming with."

I didn't look at him, too afraid of him seeing the absolute mortification on my face. Instead, I cleared my throat and nodded. "Cool."

Dad furrowed his brows and gave Scottie a sympathetic look. "She's usually a lot nicer than this I swear."

An arm rested on the back of the booth behind me, and I inched toward the table as Scottie spoke. "It's no biggie Coach. We have lots of time to get to know each other."

"You have no idea," Dad said under his breath.

The server came back with our drinks, and I took three large gulps of my skinny margarita and ignored the look of horror dad was giving me. There was no way I was confessing that Scottie and I had already met, because he'd ask questions he wouldn't like the answers to. Then I'd either get put with another guy on the team or I'd be forced to live with Dad. Could I live on my own? Of course, I was a strong independent woman who could do things like kill spiders and remember to put gas in my car before the light came on.

However, when I told my dad I was moving back to town, I was met with an offer I couldn't turn down. Live with a rcommate for a year to get acclimated—Dad's term for being watched over—and he would buy me a house. Who was I to turn down such an opportunity in this economy?

I loved him with my whole heart—but he picked the worst possible person to stick me with.

Dad crossed his hands together and sighed. "Now there's something I need to discuss with the both of you."

"Shoot Coach," Scottie said, grabbing my margarita and stealing a sip.

I smacked his hand and pulled my drink closer to my chest as I scooched as far from him as possible.

"As you're well aware Scottie, your name has been mentioned quite a lot on social media recently." Dad's brows furrowed. "And I will not have a repeat of what happened with Case a couple years ago. Do you understand?"

Sipping on my drink, my eyes went between the two men as my brain tried to understand what he was talking about. What happened with Case?

Scottie leaned back in the booth and crossed his arms. "That was totally different though. This time it's people being gossips. Nothing will come of it."

A few weeks before the wedding, a popular gossip column put out a piece that criticized men's ability to sleep around without consequences while women who did the same thing were subject to ridicule. Which was right, it wasn't fair.

Scottie wasn't called out in particular, but a jaded ex-hookup shared the article to her page and called him out. Then other people started chiming in—the list of names started with Scottie and only grew from there.

Dad shook his head. "That was what Case thought, and you saw firsthand how that played out. I refuse to let another one of my star players have a media scandal. So we're going to change your image."

"I don't need to change anything," Scottie said sternly.

"What would he need to change?" I asked, too entrapped in the drama to care about anything else.

Dad looked at me and my stomach bottomed out. The way his brows tilted inward, the way his mouth puckered a little at the ends. He only looked at me like that when he was about to deliver news I didn't want to hear.

I braced myself.

"Well Briar, he needs a girlfriend. Someone he can have on his arm in public to deter the rumors that he's a heartless womanizer." Dad pinned Scottie with a pointed stare.

Scottie laughed. "How exactly do you propose I get a girlfriend, Coach? I have a lot of numbers in my phone but none of them are relationship material. That's coming from them too."

Dad dragged his gaze to me and my skin went cold.

"No," I said. "There is no way I'm going to p-pretend to date him."

"Wow okay," Scottie mumbled from beside me, taking another sip of my drink.

"Listen. Both of you." Dad reached out and took my hands in his. "I'm willing to offer you something I think you'll enjoy. An exclusive, insider piece with the team, you can attend all practices, have access to film tapes, and even learn what toilet paper the guys use before games."

A ringing noise filled my head as I understood what my dad was offering—a chance to learn what made the Peaks, the *Peaks*. My sports blog was more of an opinion piece, I reviewed games and talked through wins and losses in a way the average, non-sporty person could understand. Every so often I would be hired to attend in person games and interview smaller sports teams, but what my dad was offering was huge. It could change the directory of my career—I could have the chance to work with the NHL network if everything went well. I'd get the chance to interview the best of the best hockey players, and maybe I could get the chance to cross into other sports, like basketball or football.

"Wait. You're proposing I date your daughter?" Scottie asked.

Dad grumbled. "Technically you'd only be dating her in public, so it wouldn't be real. But yes, essentially that's exactly what I'm proposing. The media will see you with a girlfriend and the rumors won't have any weight to them. The longer you stay single, the harder it will be to fix this problem later on if it blows up."

Dad fumbled with his napkin and then looked at me with furrowed brows before he cleared his throat. "Since you're going to be living together, and considering what I just said, we need to talk about something else."

I knew where this conversation was headed.

The safe sex talk.

I had to leave.

Dad opened his mouth, but I beat him to the punch. "I have to pee."

Both men looked at me with blank expressions, and I had to poke Scottie in the side so he could give me room to leave the booth. I finished off my margarita for good measure because I wasn't certain I'd be back. We'd see how I felt after my bathroom breakdown.

I tried to keep my face neutral as I brushed against Scottie's bicep. I couldn't give him any reason to let him think I was hung up on him. Which I wasn't, not at all—

I'd gotten plenty of average orgasms from one-night stands. Granted, the one he gave me wasn't average.

There was a mother and her young daughter when I entered the bathroom, and I waited until they left before dramatically throwing myself into a stall and leaning against the door. How in the ever-loving hell did I end up in this situation?

Didn't dad have someone else I could pretend to date? An equipment manager? A janitor? I would settle for anyone else on the team so long as it wasn't Scottie.

For half a second, I considered moving back in with my mom. I mean, she furnished an empty bedroom in her home when I told her I'd been accepted to an Irish university as an international student. If I moved back in with her she wouldn't complain. Maybe I could find a nice Irish man and get a green card.

Right?

The door opened and I was so busy rubbing my temples that the deep voice almost made me scream.

"Briar?"

I turned and slammed the stall door open, then glared at Scottie with burning cheeks. "This is the ladies' room, you can't be in here."

"If you're worried about me getting caught, don't worry, I stuck a closed for cleaning sign on the door, we're fine," he said with that wide smile of his. "And your dad thinks my mom called and that's why I stepped away. So we can have this little chat without him getting suspicious."

I crossed my arms and kept my gaze on those perfect red curls of his. "What makes you think I even want to talk to you?"

"Cause you're blushing. I feel like that's a dead giveaway."

"I am flushed because of that margarita, it has nothing to do with you," I argued. He chuckled and damn it, it sounded nice. "What do you want to do?" I asked.

His brows furrowed. "What do you mean?"

"What do you mean, what do I mean? You can't possibly tell me you're considering a fake dating arrangement so my dad can navigate a potential PR scandal. That's ridiculous."

Scottie's face went solemn before he looked at the floor. "I've seen what those scandals can do to people. If your dad is asking me to do this then I'm more than willing, but if you're not up for it, I'll find someone else."

I leaned against the wall. "Does this have anything to do with what my dad said about Case? What happened?"

"Oh, just ex-girlfriend stuff. Basil was called a lot of nasty things online after Case tried to handle things on his own," Scottie said. "But that doesn't really matter right now. Are you going to pretend to be my girlfriend or not?"

I again thought about what it would mean for my career, having access to one of the best teams in the NHL. I sighed and dropped my head.

Scottie ran a hand through his curls. "Did you know? Who I was at the wedding?" he asked, his voice small.

I nodded, well aware of the churn in my stomach.

"Why didn't you tell me?"

"Honestly I didn't think I'd run into you again, and I was curious," I said, my cheeks burning.

He let out a rough chuckle. "Great. I slept with my coach's daughter. Do you know how messed up that is?

That's like number one on how to get on a shit list. And it goes against the rules of being an asshole too."

I scrunched my nose and looked at the floor, weighting my options. On one hand, I'd be forced to pretend I'd gotten over my aversion to athletes. Which, despite our night together, I haven't.

On the other hand though, I'm being offered a once in a lifetime opportunity. A fast track to achieving my dreams and I'd be stupid to turn it down. Maybe, just maybe this could work.

"I think there's other rules on what goes against being an asshole, but whatever, let's just do it." I looked at him and blinked. "Well not *it* again, but the fake dating thing in public. We can make it work."

Scottie grinned and took a step closer, he was officially crowding me, and I couldn't focus on anything but the faint smell of lemon and linen that wafted off of him. I swallowed as I peered up at him and those perfect teeth of his.

"Just for the record Clover, if you ever want to get in my bed again, all you gotta do is ask. Pretty girls are always welcome."

There was a moment of peace that suffocated the room, but it only lasted the three seconds from those words coming out of his mouth and my foot stomping on his. He let out a pained "oof" but I didn't look back to make sure he was okay.

There was no way I was going to sleep with him again, it didn't matter how many times I had replayed our night together in my mind. Our night would remain a memory and nothing more.

———

Dad placed the last moving box in my new room while I made the bed, I changed the grey cotton sheets for my satin pink ones. The fabric felt cool against my palm as I soothed out the last few wrinkles.

"You really didn't have to help, I could have gotten it," I said.

He placed his hands against his lower back and arched. "I know you could have, but as your dad I'm obligated to help with any and all heavy lifting."

"You're supposed to be working though." I flung myself back onto the bed and stared at the flat white ceiling. Dad was supposed to be getting ready for the Peaks's game tonight, doing press interviews and making sure the guys were ready. Scottie initially offered to help me move my things, but I declined. If I was going to commit myself to another hockey player, then I needed the most prep as I could get.

The meeting at the diner seemed like it happened yesterday, not earlier this week. I still wasn't ready to pretend to be a girlfriend. My last relationship didn't exactly leave me feeling great about my relationship skills.

But nevertheless, I was going to persevere and reward myself with an unlimited sushi buffet when everything was over.

Dad laid on the bed next to me, folding his hands on his stomach. "You're more important than work."

"You know that's not true," I turned my head and smiled. "But thanks for trying to make me feel better."

"If you ever have kids you'll figure out that I'm not lying kiddo," his chest inflated as he continued to stare at the ceiling. "Will you be at the game? You know you can get the best seat in town, right behind the team."

I shouldn't, and not because I wanted to avoid Scottie,

but I had too much to unpack. Dad turned to face me, and the softness in his eyes, the slight tension between his brows made it impossible to reject his offer.

So, I pushed down my hesitation and smiled. "I'll be there."

scottie

A child cried when a worker told them the soft serve machine was down for cleaning, and another enthusiastically asked for a cup of pistachio flavored ice cream.

"Are you sure you're not just being dramatic?" Townes asked from across the table.

"Oh please, when have I ever been known to be dramatic?" I asked before shoving a spoonful of ice cream into my mouth, bringing forth a brain freeze so strong I thought I was going to explode. On the outside, however, I played it off pretty well. Townes wasn't looking at me any different than usual.

I had called an emergency meeting with the guys, we needed to discuss what happened the other morning at the restaurant. The fact Briar's dad was wanting me to pull off a PR stunt, and the fact I fucking *slept* with his daughter. If coach ever found out, then he'd make sure I signed with a different team when the season was over, and that was the last thing I wanted. The idea of leaving my teammates and my friends gave me heartburn.

Case and I had a game tonight, and I needed their help

to tell me how to be a boyfriend before then. If I was dragged into a postgame interview there was a very real chance I'd be asked about what was being said about me online. Not that I had looked, or asked. What people assumed about me wasn't any of my business, but it was affecting how the team looked, and I hated that things had come to that.

The reporters would also ask about my current dating life, and that was going to send me for a loop. How did I talk about a woman I slept with once? I couldn't very well tell them how great her boobs fit in my hands—maybe I could say something cheesy like I liked her smile.

I didn't know the first thing about how to act in a committed relationship, and it was going to show the second I opened my mouth to talk about Briar.

Was it wise to ask my two best friends who had gotten their wives after doing stupid shit? Of course it was, things worked out for them in the end.

Case shoved a spoon into his ice cream with a scowl on his face. I told him Basil wasn't allowed to come to this all-boys meeting and the lovestruck guy had been pouting the entire time.

"You're objectively the most dramatic person on the team dude. The only person who's got you beat is Hayley, and she's nine," Case said, looking at me from beside Townes.

I shook my head. "You'd be dramatic too if your one-night stand turned fake girlfriend ended up being Warner's daughter. There's a lot that can go wrong, and not to mention he wants us to put on a show. I don't know how you managed that thing with Aubrey."

Aubrey was Case's ex-*something*. They knew each other before Case signed on the team, and when she moved to

Denver she reached out for a favor. Being seen together helped skyrocket her modeling career, and while they never dated, she took Case not wanting to help her after their year-long agreement personally. Basil ended up being caught up in the drama when Case tried to solve things on his own.

The poor guy thought he lost her for a minute there.

What Warner was asking of me and Briar was different though—Case and Aubrey attended events together but never did anything to confirm they were an item. A casual touch here and there, lunch at a fancy restaurant so photos could be taken. Briar and I were expected to act like we were in love, her dad made that very clear when we left the bathroom and went back to the table.

Case shook his head. "To be honest, it would have been easier if I went to Warner for help and was honest with Basil. So speaking from experience, just do what he's asking. Don't make it weird either, or you'll have more problems on your plate."

"Yeah, a fake girlfriend isn't the worst that could have come out of the situation," Townes said.

I sighed. "You know, just because your little fake marriage ended up becoming a real one doesn't mean anything good is going to happen for my fake relationship. Also, I'm still upset that you didn't say anything that morning you saw her walk downstairs!" I pointed a finger at him before shoving another spoonful of ice cream into my mouth. Townes and Case had met Briar a few times before, and it wasn't cool of him to not say anything when she did the walk of shame.

"Sure, it wasn't my best moment. But honestly I wanted to see how things would have played out. I planned on telling you, but this whole thing with Coach happened first," he said.

I dropped my head into my hands. "I'm probably going to fuck something up, and then she's going to tattle to her dad. I'll be shipped off to the East Coast and will never see you guys again."

Case and Townes both blinked as I spiraled.

"With how you treat women at parties, I find it very hard to believe you've never had a girlfriend." Townes crossed his tattooed arms and leaned back.

Growing up, I was taught to treat women like they were unicorns, rare, magical, and needed to be treasured. It wasn't until I grew up that I realized some treasures felt nice in my hands and I wanted to experience that as much as I could. So of course I treated women like the beautiful humans they were.

For the night or two we were together anyway.

"I've had two girlfriends actually, but they were short things in middle and high school. I've evolved my game, and the evolution process was not done with long-term intimacy in mind," I said.

It was much easier to please someone for a night when the expectations were easy to follow. Woo her, make her come, and feed her before coming up with an excuse for why she couldn't stay.

Easy peasy.

"Anyway, I need you guys to tell me what to do. What do girlfriends like? Flowers? Do I touch her butt at the grocery store?" I asked.

"I still don't know why *we* are the ones you want advice from," Townes said.

I laughed as my hands slammed on the table a little harder than necessary. "Are you serious? Case fell head over heels for Basil despite the fact she was going to tear him a new one when they first met." I finished my bowl of ice cream and pointed at Townes. "And *you* totally had a crush on Hollis while she was still dating that other guy. What was his name? Reggie?"

The furrow between his brows softened and a smirk pulled on his lips. "Yeah, Reggie."

"See? If you guys could make it work, then you can tell me what to do. Please." I curled my fingers toward me, urging the both of them to offer advice. "I'm ready to listen."

Townes shook his head. "You're overthinking this, like, a lot. Hold her hand around people, make her laugh. That's really all you have to do to make people think you're together."

"Or if she's like Basil and doesn't like being touched, then show affection in other ways. The point is, so long as the camera thinks you're in love, you'll be fine," Case said.

Pretend to be in love. That was all I had to do.

I grabbed my empty ice cream cup and gave the guys a nod of determination. "Next time you both see me, me and Briar are going to be in the best fake relationship you've ever seen."

I slid out of the booth and headed toward the door. There wasn't enough time to talk to Briar before the game, but I knew I'd see her after, and we were going to put on the best performance of our lives.

briar

"And this is where the team meets before the games and during half time. It's not much, but it's enough," Dad said as he led Danny and I through the locker room.

My best friend and I were in shock as we took in the smooth wooden lockers with heavy duty combination locks. The carpet on the floor displayed the team's logo and the walls were the same color as the blue on their jerseys. Danny looked at me, his bald head reflecting the lights above us, and raised his brows. I knew what he was thinking—that he still couldn't believe my dad was a coach in the big leagues. We met when I was five and he was six. Danny was on my dad's first little league team and we became fast friends.

Danny ran his tattooed hands down his suspenders and let out a low whistle. "Wow Mr. Warner, this is really *really* cool to see."

"Thanks Danny. You know it's not too late to work toward a professional career," Dad said with a wink.

"No thanks. That shoulder injury in high school put me out of the running for anything more physical than lifting a milk frother, but if something changes you'll be the first to know."

Danny had opened a Brew & Go, a new coffee shop a few months ago, the back of it was a huge gaming area, which his business partner and boyfriend ran. People hosted their Dungeons & Dragons campaigns there, they also had a huge variety of board games to choose from—it was the perfect place for competitive nerds.

Dad rubbed his hands together and took one last look around before smiling at us. "Well I've got to get a few more things ready before the game starts. Feel free to hang out back here until then, or take the chance and go find your seats. Either way I'll see you guys after the game, oh and Bri?" He gave me a pointed look. "Remember what we talked about earlier," he said before walking away.

Yes, I remembered.

Make sure you two look like you're in love. You have to make this relationship believable.

We decided on grabbing popcorn before going to find our seats. I wasn't expecting to run into anyone since they weren't checking tickets yet, so I almost jumped out of my skin when I was grabbing my food and an eerily familiar, rough voice called my name.

"Briar? Is that you?"

While I wasn't facing Danny head on, I could tell that his jaw went slack right before he elbowed me in the ribs. I turned slowly, and like I was fifteen again, my breath caught and I could feel the fluttering sensation in the pit of my stomach. When I locked eyes with all too familiar brown ones, I smiled despite my reluctance.

He grinned back as he ran a hand through his brown

hair. He was exactly as I remembered him, though his features had sharpened up a little bit.

"Hey Maverick," I said with a wave.

We were high school sweethearts, and I thought we were going to be more, that was until graduation. Maverick convinced me we needed some space, to figure out who we were outside of our little teenage romance. It left me scrabbling emotionally, I couldn't figure out why it was so hard to be okay with being alone. After some therapy—morning coffee with my mom—and some tough conversations with Danny, I realized Maverick was a class A narcissist.

Somehow, I lost who I was in an attempt to make him happy while we were together. It was why I'd sworn off athletes, because if Maverick was that bad then surely all the others were too.

He walked over, but kept his distance and it sucked how my heart sank a little bit.

"Wow," he said, eyes roaming over me. "You look good Bri."

"What are you doing here? I thought you were with some team on the East Coast?" Not that I had been checking up on his hockey career or anything, but every once in a while, I liked to see if he signed on with another team.

Maverick shook his head. "Nah. I hurt my knee pretty bad a couple years ago, so no more hockey for me."

"Oh, I'm sorry to hear that," I said

Despite how I viewed him, the sentiment was real. Maverick had gotten lucky—with the help of my dad— and signed with a professional team after graduation. It was a shame to hear he had to quit so early in his career, but hockey was a brutal sport and some guys got the short end of the stick.

"So are you here to watch the game?" Danny chimed in, sipping on his soda.

Maverick shook his head. "Nah, I'm actually the equipment manager. Your dad helped me out when I got injured and was too stubborn to leave hockey completely. Anyway, it was nice chatting, but I've got to make sure all the guys are good to go. I'll catch you two later," he said with a wave as he headed toward the locker rooms.

Danny and I headed to our seats, and I tuned him out when he went on a rampage of how much he still didn't like Maverick. In high school they always butted heads, he claimed I was too good for Maverick, and he didn't like the way he treated me. I used to think he was overreacting because he only saw us together at school and when we'd all hang out at hockey games or other school events. But now that I knew better, I felt bad for putting my best friend in an uncomfortable situation.

A tiny thought caught my attention; what would Maverick think of Scottie? They worked together, and he was probably well aware of his *activities*. Would he be jealous we were together? Maybe I could get something else out of this little arrangement besides securing a job with the network as a sports writer.

"Earth to Bri," Danny said with a wave of his hand in front of my face. "You went into a daze, everything okay?"

I flashed him a smile as people started to fill the seats around us. "I'm fine, just looking forward to this whole thing being over. I'm thinking tacos after?"

Danny ran a hand through his beard—if he wasn't bald, he'd have amazing volume, I was sure of it—and shook his head with a grin. "If I say yes to tacos, will you at least tell me who on the team you banged? I've been through the roster like ten times and none of them look like your type."

I wondered if he was looking at the old roster. I'd sent him or the new one—because there was *definitely* someone on the team who was my type. Not that it mattered much.

"Maybe you aren't looking hard enough," I said with a shrug. "We can make it a game, if you successfully guess who it was then I'll dog sit for a whole weekend."

Danny's eyes widened. "Wait really? You'd do that?"

Danny and his partner were the proud owners of an elderly, medically complex chihuahua and rarely left the house for more than a few hours. They were understandably wary of strangers taking care of Mr. Moo, but I'd gone with Danny to pick him up when we were in middle school. That dog was just as much my baby as it was his, and if I could help Danny and his partner take time for themselves, then I'd do it.

"You gotta guess though," I said with a wink.

Danny gave me a curt nod and turned his focus to the athletes on the ice. Everyone was in various stretching positions, and I made it a point to look everywhere except at the number eighteen—that was Scottie's.

"That guy?" Danny asked as he pointed toward two guys, Scottie and someone I recognized as Riley. They were both forwards and were skating around the rink, shoving each other and throwing their heads back in laughter.

I bit my lip and was too slow to shake my head no when Danny elbowed my side. "I knew it! Which one huh?"

As if Scottie could sense someone was talking about

him, he stopped and turned in our general direction. We were too high in the stands to make eye contact so I wasn't worried about him seeing me.

Danny pointed at Riley with a questioning brow. "Him?"

I shook my head and glanced at the jumbotron at the same time it decided to pan across Scottie. He grinned when a very loud group of women in the crowd cheered.

"Oh my god. That guy? Who is he? I didn't see him on the roster!" Danny looked like he was going to keel over from excitement.

I nodded. "His name is Scottie."

"Oh I like that name, *Scottie*. It rolls off the tongue nicely."

I sipped on my cheap beer. "He's my new roommate too. I forgot to mention that earlier didn't I? Oops."

"You're *what*? Roommate? The one your dad set you up with? Does he know?"

As much as I loved Danny, he could be the tiniest overdramatic at the worst of times, so I placed a hand over his mouth and scrunched my nose when he licked my hand like he did when we were little.

"Ew," I said as I rubbed my hand on my pants.

"Don't act all surprised. Now, tell me everything! How'd you find out?"

I bit the inside of my cheek. "My dad cornered me at a diner, then Scottie showed up. Oh, also before I forget"—I took a long drink of my beer—"Scottie and I are uh dating. Kind of I guess. My dad said something about cleaning up Scottie's image, so I was wrangled into the mess. On the bright side though, I'm going to get exclusive access to the team for my blog." I smiled.

Danny's mouth dropped and I was worried for a

moment that he'd stopped breathing until a loud buzzer went off. The game started and we became too engrossed in the game to continue any kind of conversation. I'd forgotten how much fun hockey games were, it had been years since the last one I'd gone to. Danny and I cheered from the stands, and even though I would never admit it, I might have cheered a little harder for a particular redhead.

scottie

I lived for praise.

When I learned how to ride a bike, my dad took me for ice cream, and when I scored the winning goal in my little league hockey team, my parents took all of us out for pizza and boasted that they were raising the next best player to ever hit the ice. So was my ego bigger than my dick?

Almost. But I knew how to be humble when it mattered. On the ice wasn't the place though, any time a teammate scored or our goalie made an amazing save, I was the first one there to give kudos. The times I scored the winning goal or made a last-minute decision to help our defense was where I thrived. I skated on the high the crowd gave me until the final buzzer rang and I was able to carry the adrenaline to postgame interviews and parties.

Tonight was different though as the crowd blurred around me, like someone was watching me with a heated intensity I didn't recognize. Every so often I'd get a feeling on my neck; a single woman who came because she heard

I'd be at a party, someone's wife who was thinking what her life would be like had she made different decisions and didn't marry a used car salesman. Those stares I was used to, but this one had my head turning to scan the crowd as Riley raced down to the opposing team's goal.

Once, twice—there. A head of fiery red hair standing behind the plexiglass close to our bench where her dad and the rest of the team sat. I spun away when someone called my name, and focused on traveling down the ice with Riley who had the puck.

We fought against the Panters defense, tiring ourselves as we tried to spot an opening. At the last second Riley took the shot, and when the buzzer rang, signaling the winning goal, we dog piled on him.

Cheers from the crowd roared around us as we split and went to shake hands with the other team. We then went to the locker rooms, and I was ready for a speedy shower so I could avoid being dragged into a postgame interview. That dream died though when I found Coach waiting for me when I was done. His arms were crossed and he stared at me with a raised brow.

"Where are you going?" he asked, looking at my duffle bag I had slung over my shoulder.

"Oh, uh. I was going to meet up with Briar," I said, trying to step around him.

He shook his head and placed a hand on my shoulder, pushing slightly to spin me around. We walked side by side to an interview room and my stomach churned.

"All you have to do is say you met a lovely woman and hit it off with her. They're not going to pry for more information, and if they do, just redirect them to Case. He'll talk about Basil until he's blue in the face and the media loves hearing his little love story."

We walked into the media room, reporters sat in foldout chairs and were waiting for me to fill the empty seat beside Case. Riley was there too since he made the winning shot, and I hoped they'd ask him all their questions.

If only life worked that way. After five minutes, Deborah Adams—an older woman whom I recognized from previous postgame interviews—smiled at me.

"Mr. Lancaster, it's no secret your name is being circulated around online recently, and that you've been rumored to have been spending time with a woman. Are the two related? Did this mystery woman have any impact on how you played tonight?"

If there was one thing Deborah loved, it was gossip.

I ran my hands against my jeans before flashing a confident smile. "What people say about me online is all opinion, and as for this supposed woman you're referring too, well let's just say that not every part of my life needs media attention."

"Is she your girlfriend then?" Deborah asked with a smirk.

My smile widened as I felt Case eyeing me. "Yes actually, she is, and I won't be answering any further questions regarding my relationship."

The questions that followed were directed at Case and Riley, and I sat back with my hands on the table and let them speak. There was nothing else for me to add to the conversation, they'd gotten what they wanted from me, and I had done what Coach asked.

We stayed in that interview room for another ten minutes. Case met Basil outside of the media room and Riley headed toward the parking lot, ready to head to the bar to celebrate.

Coach gave me a solid nod when I walked past him, grateful he was satisfied with how I handled the line of questioning, I relaxed my shoulders. I exited the long hallway that led toward the front of the building and my eyes gravitated toward the pretty redhead standing near the front doors.

Briar was talking to some bald guy covered in tattoos, her back toward me and something prickled up my back. Who was that? Was he making her uncomfortable?

Last year when I promised Coach I'd watch after his daughter I meant it, and I was ready to beat this guy into the ground if he was bothering her. But something happened as I stalked closer, his eyes widened and he tapped her arm in a frantic motion. She looked down where he was touching her and I watched him say something, then she turned around. Her clothes were tight enough to make me wonder if her dad saw her, because the jeans and lace top left nothing to the imagination. Fuck had she been wearing that the whole game?

In front of everyone?

"Hey Clover," I said as I reached her and put my arm over her bare shoulders.

She shrugged me off. "Hi."

"Oh my gosh! I'm Danny. Such a huge fan," the bald guy said. He wore dark jeans and yellow suspenders, the well-groomed handlebar mustache really tied his whole look together. Who was he to Briar?

I reached for his outstretched hand and smiled. "Nice to meet you. So uh, how do you know Clover here?"

"Oh. *Clover?*" He looked at Briar and wiggled his brows, it was cute seeing her cheeks go red at the teasing. Before she said anything, he put his hands in his pockets and held my gaze. "We grew up together, met at my first hockey game in first grade. She used to draw on my hockey sticks."

A laugh escaped me and I threw my head back. The image of a little redheaded Briar consumed my mind—her drawing on hockey sticks, helmets, and yelling at her dad's feet.

Cute.

I cleared my throat and nudged my elbow into her side since she was adamant about not looking at me, which I didn't understand. I was handsome as hell and well—she knew what was in my pants.

"We're all going out for drinks, you two should come."

Danny's eyes lit up. "Oh my gosh! An after party?"

"Yeah, at a bar downtown, nothing crazy."

Danny looked at Briar and placed his hand in a prayer position under his chin. "Please can we go? Ronny is working tonight, and I'll be bored if you make me go home."

She scoffed. "You have work tomorrow."

"So? I'm my own boss. If I show up tomorrow with a hangover no one's going to care. Well maybe Joanna, but she's been working up to be a manager so I'm kind of expecting that from her." Danny waved a hand.

Briar flashed those pretty eyes up at me before dropping her shoulders. I took one look at her soft skin, remembered what laid beneath that dark fabric, and grabbed a hoodie from my duffle bag. I placed it haphazardly over her shoulders and pointed toward the parking lot.

"If you don't want to, that's fine. Did you drive together? Do you need a ride home?" I asked before steering us to the parking lot.

Briar clung onto Danny as they walked beside me. He

was smiling at her, his hand resting against hers where it laid on his arm.

"I drove us tonight and I can take her home if you need," he said.

I shook my head. "No, that's fine, I'll take her."

"You're not going?" Briar asked with furrowed brows.

If I was being honest with myself, I didn't want to go. Not before Briar and I had the chance to start on a clean slate. Our situation started on a high note and quickly tumbled down a gigantic hill. We needed to figure out how to get ourselves out of this hole without trampling over one another. It was obvious earlier that what Coach offered Briar for being my fake girlfriend was important to her, and while I didn't care for my image as much as he needed me to, I wasn't going to ruin the opportunity for her.

briar

This night was not going how I pictured.

First, I listened in on Scottie's postgame interview and my stomach did a weird flip thing when he answered that reporter—the traitor. Then I ran into Maverick again after the interview and had to make an excuse as to why I didn't want to bring my *boyfriend* on a double date with him and his new girlfriend. By the time I saw Scottie walk out of the athletic area all I wanted to do was go home and rot on the couch.

So thank God he was able to read me and offered to take me home.

We drove home in silence. He drummed his fingers against the steering wheel and didn't look my way once.

When he pulled into the driveway I got out and darted inside, rushing upstairs to shed out of my constricting clothes. I tossed Scottie's hoodie on my bed and opted for my favorite sleeping gown—my grandmother put me onto them—and then traded my contacts for glasses. When I got downstairs, Scottie was nowhere to be seen. Assuming he was busy with whatever man stuff he had to do, I wandered into the kitchen. The pantry was fully stocked, but not with snacks, with ingredients. I tried my luck with the fridge and found a small cup of yogurt. When I grabbed a spoon Scottie returned, only to stop and stare from the opposite end of the kitchen island.

"What?" I asked. "Are you mad I took your yogurt? I was going to Venmo you to make up for it. I'm just hungry and—"

"What are you wearing?" he asked with a stricken expression.

I glanced down at the yellow flower-patterned fabric. "My nightgown?"

"I—" He started laughing. "I'm s-sorry, I've just never seen someone below the age of eighty wear one of those things."

I set my yogurt cup on the counter harder than necessary and crossed my arms. "Oh what, you only see women wear nightgowns when they're scratchy and see-through?"

He kept laughing and I rolled my eyes. When I finished my snack, he made a show of wiping a tear from his eyes. "Oh wow, sorry that—I needed that laugh. Today's been weird."

"You're telling me," I mumbled.

There was an awkward pause between us as I waited for him to say something, wondering why my dad thought this was a good idea. Was it believable to others that I landed someone like Scottie? He was handsome, had decent manners and knew his way around a woman's body, but were we even in the same league? I liked to think my self-esteem was decently high, but something nagged in the back of my brain, telling me there was no reason it should be.

I should just move back in with my mom.

When Scottie remained quiet, I straightened my back and put on my metaphorical big girl pants—I hated pants. "Do you want to watch a movie? We can snack and chat," I said.

He gave me a pointed look through hooded lashes and nodded. "Are we going to talk about everything?"

I nodded.

"I'll get the popcorn then," he said before turning his back on me.

I darted to the couch, not knowing what to put on yet somehow landing on *The Proposal*. Scottie landed on the couch soon after the opening credits with a bowl of popcorn, bags of various gummy candy, and chips.

"I'm pretty sure I know the answer to this, but you can never be too sure. Have you ever had a fake boyfriend?" Scottie asked as he reached for a bag of gummies.

I laid back on the couch, careful to keep my distance from him. "No. In fact I've only had one boyfriend back in high school."

"I find it hard to believe a pretty girl like you hasn't had a boyfriend in what, four years?"

He offered me a gummy, and I took it. "Five actually, and one could say the same about you. How is it that you've built up this image of a playboy when you're totally boyfriend material?" I asked.

Scottie shook his head. "You don't know that I'm boyfriend material."

Did he not think he was? After the night we met—how he made sure I stayed warm, danced with me in the snow —and even tonight when he offered to bring me home after he saw I didn't want to go out. Those actions were very much boyfriend things.

Scottie leaned back, his shirt bunched above the waist-line of his pants and the sight of skin sent heat through me.

"I don't mind you know," he said, adjusting his position on the couch, the movement causing his shirt to lift up. "I'm not going to complain about our situation if that's what you're worried about. We both have too much at stake for either of us to mess anything up."

He didn't seem like the kind of person who had anything at stake. It made me wonder how true his words were, but I appreciated them regardless.

"Thank you," I said, looking at him.

Scottie held my gaze for a long moment before his expression turned serious. "I don't know if it makes a difference, but had I known you were Warner's daughter I swear I never would have made a move on you." His eyes narrowed as if he was questioning his words. "Actually, I take that back, I totally would have, but I wouldn't have acted on it."

I bit my bottom lip as a distraction from the tingles that erupted in the base of my spine. Memories of his mouth on mine, on my skin, it was too much, and as much as I should have cared, I didn't. I wasn't going to fall for him, but that didn't mean I couldn't think of how good we were together.

He winked. "At least you went home with the hottest one too, cause man, you sleeping with anyone else? You're too good for those fools."

"But not you?" I quipped before reaching for some more popcorn.

He shook his head. "Me too, especially me. You gave my ego a huge confidence boost agreeing to spend the night with me, and for that I am forever grateful."

"A man like you needs an ego boost? What has the world come to?" I smiled and adjusted my glasses.

It was a somewhat serious question; men like Scottie didn't require external validation or ego boosts to move through life. Those that did listened to alpha male podcasts and had receding hairlines by the age of twenty-five.

Scottie reached over and grabbed a free strand of hair between his fingers. I didn't pull away from him, didn't want to, nor felt the need, which was the opposite of how I should have reacted.

"I'm secretly a very fragile man Briar, you'll learn that soon enough."

I rolled my eyes. "Could have fooled me."

"Well that's because we don't know each other and I'm determined to change that," he said before jumping over the couch and grabbing some drinks from the fridge. He handed me a beer and settled back into his spot. "When do you want to start?"

My brows creased. "Start what?"

"Bonding of course. How else will we have the best fake relationship? I think we should get to know each other so whenever anyone asks questions we don't look stupid."

"That's a valid point, but are you absolutely sure? We can make this easy and just memorize notes or something."

I was worried Scottie was going to give himself whiplash with how hard he nodded. His mouth was tight when he looked at me, his brows furrowed with a stern intensity. "As sure as I was when I convinced my niece to call her other uncle Casey instead of Case. She still does it to this day by the way, super cute. Now I propose we start bonding tomorrow, and we can talk more about our little arrangement, maybe at a bar to liven things up?"

Mentally I went through everything I had to do tomorrow, which wasn't much. The only thing urgent was to get a list of questions ready for when I showed up at Scottie's next practice. I still had to talk to my dad about the logistics; if any topics were off limits, if there was anyone who was a PR nightmare, and other technical stuff.

I nodded. "That sounds good. But if you want to start earlier, maybe you can join me for my morning run?"

The smile he gave me sent butterflies loose in my stomach I was going to need a mantra—*I will not* actually *fall for Scottie Lancaster.*

scottie

Briar was trying to kill me.

Sure my muscles looked great in compression shirts, I could easily move heavy furniture, and they looked amazing in the right lighting when I sent spicy pictures. When it came to any activity involving cardio though? I was useless, and not for a lack of trying, but my California lungs had never fully acclimated to the change in elevation.

Which left me sprawled out on my front lawn, sweat dripping down my face despite the cool temperature. Why couldn't Briar run in the warmer months? Was the middle of February prime running time?

"If you don't get up, you might freeze out here. Let's go inside," Briar said as she held out her hand for me to take.

She wore a sea blue running set, with a matching thick headband that covered her ears. Her red hair was up in a single braid, and she had her contacts in; I'll admit I'd spent more time looking at her butt during our run than focusing on my breathing which was probably why it felt like I was dying more than usual.

I had no regrets.

Once inside, I started making breakfast and Briar went upstairs. She didn't come back down until the food was ready; her hair freshly washed and her laptop in hand.

"That smells really good," she said, coming to stand next to me.

I flipped the last pancake onto an empty plate and handed it to her. "Hope you're not one of those runners who only eats rabbit food to stay in shape."

Briar looked up at me with a smile. "Keep it up and I'll make sure you're eating like a rabbit too. Thanks for cooking by the way," she said with a slight pink hue to her cheeks before she walked to the table. I didn't think anything of it as I made my plate and got us both glasses of juice.

"So are you still up for some hanging out today? Al's opens at noon and I figured we could get some burgers for lunch since the bar doesn't have the best food options. Unless, of course, your rabbit instincts are drawing you to something else?"

Briar nodded as she took a huge bite of food. I busied myself until she was ready to talk, scrolling on my phone and answering the booty calls I'd ignored last night. Since news broke out I had a girlfriend, it seemed like *everyone* decided now was prime time to get into my pants. They asked if the relationship was serious, or promised they'd keep their beds warm for my inevitable break up.

Which was rude because I was a taken man and how dare they assume I was the kind of person to cheat. Sure I got around, but that didn't mean I didn't have morals, ethics, and standards. In college, I never felt the need to have a girlfriend, I was too busy with classes and hockey to have a relationship. Then when I signed with the Peaks,

most of the women who surrounded me were more interested in my bank account than me as a person. It was
easier to have a history of satisfied one-night stands than
a history of heartbroken women I couldn't provide for
emotionally.

"I've got some prep to do for tomorrow, but once I'm
done yeah," she said.

"Was there anything you needed help with? Any
rumors I could start to make your interviews tomorrow
be more fun?" I could totally tell her that Riley had a
hidden identity, and that Jameson, one of our defensemen,
was scared of clowns.

She shook her head and bit her lip. I stared at her as
my body warmed in a way I knew wasn't related to our
workout.

"I appreciate the offer but no thanks. I'm going to go
into this with a clean slate and little expectations." She
tapped her hands on the countertop, and I knew that was
my cue to leave.

I smiled at Briar. "Well, I'll leave you to it for now."

"You're leaving?" she asked.

"What? You're already so attached you can't stand me
being gone?"

She huffed and opened her laptop, turning away from
me. "I was hoping something else had drawn your attention so I could work all day. Oh well, I'll come find you
when I'm done and we can get going."

I threw her a quick wink before standing. "See you in a
bit Clover."

———

"You can not be serious," Briar said under her breath when we entered Al's.

At the far end of the building there sat a few guys from the team, and our team's equipment manager Maverick. I wasn't even sure they'd seen us come in yet, but Briar hung her head beside me, as if she was the recognizable one next to a six-foot-three hockey player. I was quickly mistaken when Maverick glanced in our direction. He gave us a curt nod, his body so tense I could see it from where we stood. I returned the gesture anyway before I leaned down and placed one hand on her shoulder while the other grabbed her free hand.

"Do you want to go somewhere else?" I asked, leaning in. We hadn't gone over any boundaries or *rules* for what we were doing, but she wasn't hiding the fact she didn't want to be here for some reason.

She shook her head. "No, it's fine. It's just, uh." Her eyes darted to the table and the hairs on my neck stood at attention. "Never mind. Come on, let's find a seat."

Once we were at the bar and had our drinks ordered, Briar took in a breath and faced me. Determination set in her features under the pink tint in her cheeks. I drew my finger over the back of her hand in soft, soothing motions.

"You okay?" I asked.

She nodded. "Yeah, it's just, kind of weird right?"

I shrugged.

"Okay." She set her shoulders back and took in a deep breath. "How should we go about this? Are you the touchy-feely kind of boyfriend? Or maybe you're super possessive and—"

I placed my index finger against her lips, effectively silencing her and her rambling. "Why are you trying to dictate what kind of boyfriend I should be? Shouldn't I be myself?"

Her shoulder sagged and she took three very large sips of the blue cocktail that was placed in front of her. "You're right. You should be yourself even though I'm still not confident in what that looks like, but I digress. We need to think about other things too, like rules. We need those."

I sipped on my beer. "Like?"

"Well, the house for starters. Have you lived with roommates before? Anything I should know about?" she asked, licking her bottom lip as she fluttered her lashes at me. Was it intentional?

God she was cute.

"Before you, I lived with our old goalie and his niece. I'm not going to be stingy about stuff because we're both adults, but I do ask that if you cook anything to please not leave wet food in the sink. Have you ever touched soggy bread? It's gross and I will throw up."

Her nose scrunched before she took another sip of her drink, her eyes darting to the table in the back. "The feeling is mutual. I like to buy those scented things that make the drain *not* smell like rotten food. Think you could use those?"

"Oh baby, if you look under the sink you'll see three boxes of those under there," I said with a huge grin. "I also have this thing about shoes in the house, that's a big no-no for me."

The thought of dirt being tracked inside made my skin crawl. Growing up in a large family, my parents somehow made it bigger by adding a dog. Then one turned to two, and there always seemed to be dirt inside. It wasn't the end of the world if Briar wore shoes inside, but I'd have to look into hiring a cleaning service if that was the case.

Much to my relief, Briar nodded, her brows creased together. "I can work with that."

"What about you? Anything you're picky about?"

Briar bit her bottom lip and thought for a long moment, I busied myself with the TV show playing on the outdated television above the bar. Some cowboy was getting ready for an old-fashioned showdown when Briar cleared her throat.

"I just ask that if you bring women back to the house, you're careful about it," she said with her gaze focused downward.

My brows creased together, confusion making its way into my brain. "Why do you think I'd bring other women home?" I asked.

She sucked in a breath and stared at me like I was the one being ridiculous and spouting nonsense. "Because we're not really together, and you're a man with"—she grabbed her glass and finished her drink—"needs."

I snorted, an involuntary sound that I hoped didn't draw attention. I needed Briar to understand that I was serious about what I said last night, we were in this together. Besides I wasn't going to risk anything because I was too caught up on getting my dick wet.

"Are you saying my needs are more important than yours?" I asked.

She shook her head. "No, but I just want to be courteous and not dictate what you do in your free time, in your own room. So again, so long as you're discrete about it I won't care."

This woman was—something else.

I sighed and grabbed her chin, forcing her to look at me. "Listen here Clover. As your fake boyfriend it's my job to make it look like you're in a happy relationship, and that extends to making it look like you get fucked. Regularly. So no, I will not be sneaking women into my bedroom when you're down the hall. But if you're that concerned about me getting blue balls then maybe we can add friends with benefits to the list of things you need from me."

Her cheeks turned a shade of red I hadn't seen before, and I smiled. It was impossible not to when she was looking as stunning as she was.

"Okay so house rules established, and my celibacy out in the open; what other rules do you want in place?" I asked.

Briar tilted her head as she bit her pink straw. "We only put on this act in the open. At home and at the rink we act like the single people we are, got it?"

I nodded once. "I can grope you in public where pictures will be taken but not around the team, and don't fuck you. Got it."

She clicked her tongue and rolled her eyes as she tried not to smile. "You don't have to grope me at *all*."

"Okay." I sipped my beer when something came to mind. "Oh! The event!"

"Event?" she asked.

"Yeah, there's a big charity event coming up in a couple months. You're coming right? We can make a big deal of it. I'm sure your dad would love it for me and my image. Then after we can slowly fade out our relationship."

Briar looked at the ceiling, her mouth moving as she talked to herself. "Two months? Isn't that a little short notice for a big event like that?"

"Your point?" I took a sip of her drink, my face tightened as the unpleasant taste of vodka went down my throat. When she didn't respond, I leaned on the counter and leveled her with a stare. "Here's how I see it. We show up to the gala together, it'll generate enough buzz to please the media. Then we play pretend for another couple months before calling it quits. So, four months total. Easy peasy.

Briar raised a brow. "Do you think you can manage it?"

I almost laughed. "Are you saying you don't think I can fake date you for four months? Briar, that's nothing in the grand scheme of things. Did you know one of my best friends was in a fake marriage?"

She blinked. "Oh my god."

"Yeah. But don't worry, they fell in love, and their marriage is one hundred percent real. If he can do that, then I can do this."

Briar's eyes seemed to light up as she smiled, and for a moment I wanted to freeze time. Get lost in the maps of freckles on her face, her body. Fuck I was getting hard, and all I'd done was look at her a little too hard.

Four months. I could go four months without fucking her—or anyone. It was me and my hand against the world.

briar

"Has anyone ever told you it's not polite to stare?" I asked Scottie as I sipped my coffee. I felt his eyes on me the moment I walked into the kitchen, and the feeling never went away. So either he'd been staring at me, or I was so paranoid about him staring that I was going crazy.

It was odd. Maverick used to look at me all the time, so have other men I've dated, but I've never felt so *aware* before.

When I spun around and rested against the counter I was met with Scottie smirking, shaking his head, he plunged his spoon into his cereal.

"I'm sorry but it's kind of hard not to when you're wearing those pants," he said.

With furrowed brows I glanced down at my dark purple slacks, looking for a hole or a stain I hadn't noticed before I put them on. "What's wrong with them?"

"They look good." I watched as his eyes darted to them again before he shook his head. "But are they suitable for what you're doing today?"

"Why wouldn't they be?" I asked. Today was my first

day attending a Peaks practice. I had questions lined up for a few of the players, my dad, and even people on their management team. I needed to know how the team clicked together so well, and didn't see how my slacks had anything to do with it.

"They're tight," he said, walking over and placing his bowl in the sink. "It might cause a distraction is all, so maybe you should change."

I stared at him, unsure of what to say. Most of the players on the Peaks were married or had long-term significant others. That wasn't to say they didn't have wandering eyes, but that said more about them than it did me. I crossed my arms and watched Scottie as he turned toward me.

"If you're worried about your teammates not being respectful then that's not my problem," I said.

He leaned down and smirked. "I'm not talking about them, Clover. You in those pants is a distraction for *me*, so please change. I don't feel like getting my ass chewed out by your dad because I couldn't stop staring at you."

"You're flirting," I said with furrowed brows. "Keep that stuff for when we're around people who think we're dating."

He shook his head. "Can't. I'm not sure if you know this Briar, but you have a habit of getting flustered and looking like a cute little tomato when you're caught off guard. I need to condition you to my charm before we go out in public."

Damn him and his very logical reasoning. Scottie leaned in closer, and it took everything in me to not pull away or move even closer. My brain and my lady bits wanted two very different things, and I didn't have time to argue with either of them right now.

"So please Clover, can you change your pants so your boyfriend can get through his practice unscathed?" Scottie asked with batted lashes.

I took a step toward him until we were chest to chest, he straightened, and I had to crane my neck back to look at him. His body was so warm, and I knew how soft his skin would be if I reached out and touched him. I raised myself onto my tiptoes until we were just inches apart and I was sure he stopped breathing.

"No," I whispered with a smile. I backed away and spun toward the door, making sure to sway my hips in exaggeration as I walked. "See you at practice!"

My eyes stayed on Scottie as I watched him dash across the ice, he was running drills alongside Case and Riley while I watched from the bleachers.

I'd spent most of practice on my computer finishing up an initial draft for my blog, creating an announcement for the upcoming interview with the team, and doing some research into their next game. They would be traveling and I needed to study up on their opposing teams so I could be prepared for whatever story I needed to write.

"Hi. It's Briar right?" someone asked, pulling me from my work. I looked to my left and furrowed my brows. The woman looked familiar with her dark brown hair, but I was having a hard time placing where I'd seen her.

"Yes?" I asked, moving over on the bench when she sat down.

She turned her body toward me as she took off her hoodie with the building's logo on it. "We didn't get a chance to meet at the wedding, I'm Basil."

My eyes widened as it hit me. "Oh! Gosh sorry, hi it's nice to meet you." I fumbled with my computer as I closed it and put it in my bag. "I didn't know you came to practice."

"I usually don't because it conflicts with my coaching job. But my practice ended early and I figured I'd stop by," she said with a smile. Basil looked around before leaning in and the hairs on the back of my neck stood. "I also heard that you're dating Scottie, and I wanted to see what that was about."

My first instinct was to deny it, run away and pretend I never ran into her, but that would defeat the purpose of Scottie and I's arrangement.

I smiled. "What did you want to know exactly? How we met or maybe something else a girlfriend would totally know about her boyfriend? Sorry, it's still a little new."

This wasn't starting off well. God what was I saying? She was never going to believe we were a thing, and if she didn't then the media totally wouldn't, and well—I just ruined everything. Bye bye dream job.

Basil chuckled and shook her head. "Oh! No, I know you two aren't together."

"You do? How?" I asked, my shoulders relaxing a bit.

"Case told me all about it, of course after Scottie told him," she said through a smile.

I turned toward the rink to find him on the ice, which didn't take long considering he'd taken off his helmet. Red curls were plastered to his neck, and I had to force myself to look away when he started to turn toward us.

"Of course he did," I said, staring down at my unkept fingers. I'd started picking at the skin of my thumbs again—a habit I thought I'd broken when I moved to live with Mom. It started up again after running into Maverick.

Basil was quiet when she spoke again, as if I were a scared dog she'd found on the side of the road. Okay that was me being dramatic, but it was how I felt. I didn't know how I was supposed to act about Scottie when someone asked. Maybe I should let him flirt with me—make it seem more real.

"If you don't want to talk about it, you don't have to. I get it's a little weird," she said.

I shook my head and smiled at her. "It's a little relieving if I'm being honest. I don't have anyone I can talk about this with—well, anyone who has a sane head on their shoulders."

Danny was team *fake dating* and wouldn't stop sending me videos of date ideas. He insisted he was helping, but most of the videos were of places in different countries and he offered to tag along to make sure I was doing okay.

He was delusional about me getting my happily ever after. It would—might—happen one day, just not with Scottie.

Basil smiled and scooted closer, pulling something wrapped in plastic wrap out of her pocket. "Don't tell Case, but these aren't the brownies he made. Want some?" She held out a piece. "I promise they're just as good."

I grabbed a piece and took a bite. "Oh wow. These are amazing. Where did you get them?"

"Rhonda's. Her place is down the block. Here, let's exchange numbers and I'll send you the info." Basil took out her phone the same time I did, and a moment later I got a pinned location for the cafe.

"Thanks, and uh thanks for offering to be a listening ear," I said, casting Scottie another quick glance.

"Anytime, and if Scottie is being too much or hurts your feelings, just send me a text or call. I'll come over with snacks, we'll kick him out and make fun of how our niece picks on him."

I laughed and took another bite of the brownie.

"For the record Briar," Basil said as she looked at the ice, "Scottie is one of the best guys I know. He'd never hurt a fly, and he has a huge heart. I'm not saying any of this to convince you to *actually* date him or anything, but you can trust him to not go back on his word or mess things up for you."

The words were a relief and although I didn't know Basil outside of what I'd heard about her from Scottie and Dad, I knew I could trust her. So if she said Scottie was trustworthy, then I'd hold onto those words.

A whistle blew, drawing our attention to the guys below us, they were gathered around my dad. It never got old seeing him out there, knowing he was a teenage father and worked his ass off to get to where he was today. I was immensely proud of him for being persistent about following his dreams.

"That's our cue to get down there, come on," Basil said.

I grabbed my bag and followed after her as she led me toward the locker rooms. We waited outside the doors, smiling at the guys as they walked past us. Scottie's eyes lit up when they landed on me, and I made a point to smile like a lovestruck puppy. We were around the team so it had to be believable.

Basil and I chatted while we waited—which wasn't long at all. In the middle of discussing which new release books we were looking forward to reading, two familiar arms wrapped themselves around my middle. Scottie smelled like fresh linen and men's deodorant, nothing in particular but he smelled *manly.*

I shouldn't have liked it as much as I did.

"I see you two met. Is she being nice to you Briar?" Scottie asked, the faint scruff of a beard tickling the side of my face. I didn't know the man could grow a beard, and wondered for a second if I could convince him to grow it out.

"I'm always nice," Basil said with crossed arms.

Case walked over from Scottie's direction and pulled Basil into his arms before placing a kiss on the top of her head. "Oh yeah. Always."

Scottie leaned in closer, and I let my body melt back into his. He whispered, "When they first met, Basil tore him a new one because she thought he caused a car accident involving her best friend."

I turned my head until I was looking into his eyes, my brows furrowed. "And?"

"And when she realized it was my fault she apologized and ran off. Now look at them, married and ready for little hockey player babies."

Basil whipped her head toward us and pointed a finger. "There will be no talks of babies for at *least* five years. I will not be a teen pregnancy statistic."

Scottie let me go and held up his hands. "I'm not saying you're going to get knocked up anytime soon. Just that you guys would make cute babies."

She sighed and dropped her head into Case's chest, who was smiling and shaking his head. Scottie's hand landed on my back, his thumb drew small circles as I relaxed into his touch.

"What are you two doing for the rest of the day?" Case asked.

Scottie answered before I had the chance to. "I'm taking Briar on a little date."

"Really?" Basil asked with a tense mouth. "You do know that Case and I both know this is fake right? You don't have to pretend in front of us."

"Oh I know. But Coach asked me to give the media some pictures so they could talk about how I'm reformed or some shit. That, and Maverick invited us on a double date later this week and we need to make sure we've got everything down pat. Can't give him any indication that we aren't madly in love," Scottie said, hooking a finger through my middle belt loop and pulling me toward him.

This was news to me. Us and Maverick on a double date? Scottie tugged on the waistband of my pants, forcing me to give Case and Basil a quick goodbye before I was hauled toward the parking lot. He didn't say anything, or let me go, instead he looped his index finger into the side loop of my pants. I kind of liked it, being man handled and forced to follow him, but now was *not* the time to think about whatever kinks were rearing their heads.

I didn't want to go on a double date or see Maverick if I could help it. Sure it was inevitable, but the longer we could put it off the better. Scottie dragged me toward his truck and grabbed my bag before opening the door.

"In," he said.

I crossed my arms. "No. Not until you at least tell me why you agreed to a double date with Maverick."

His brows furrowed and his gaze shot to my pants once before returning back to mine. "Do you know him?"

I supposed now was the time to tell him. I sighed and leaned against the car. "We dated back in high school and the other night after the game he invited me on a double date. I turned him down because I honestly don't care to see him more than I need to."

"Why didn't you tell me?" Scottie asked.

"Because I didn't think it was important."

Scottie didn't need to know all the details of my life, at least not yet. We were barely friends, and I hoped we could at least bond over something stupid before I told him all my issues. Those being; I got my heart broken by Maverick, I couldn't cook, and I couldn't swim.

Scottie reached out and grabbed my hand, linking our fingers together. I looked up at him and was met with a hardness in his eyes. "Do you want me to cancel? Because I can, I don't want you to be uncomfortable."

Why was he so nice?

"No it's okay. Promise," I said, giving his hand a squeeze before pulling away. "Now where are we going?"

I got in the car and waited for him to hop into the driver's seat. A giant smile was plastered on his face as he turned the car on and started out of the parking lot.

"It's a surprise," he said before reaching over and grabbing my thigh. "For my sake, can you please not wear these again to practice? I wasn't kidding earlier when I said it would cause a distraction."

I turned my head away to hide my smile. The idea of me being a distraction sounded fantastic. I needed some new clothes.

scottie

The last time I was this nervous for a date was my freshman year of high school. I was taking Sandy McAllen to the movies and I ended up falling *up* the theater steps and wasted half of the extra-large tub of popcorn. So we watched the movie in silence and had no *accidental hands touching while reaching for the popcorn* moment.

It was a bust.

I was nervous now because, well, I wanted this date to go well. Not only for my sake but for Briar's too, she was so flustered this morning, and I couldn't help but wonder when she last went out. Surely she'd dated since Maverick right? She didn't post regularly on her socials—yes I stalked her—so there was no way to tell how many people she'd dated. And not that it mattered, but I wanted to be the best person she's been with even if it wasn't real.

"I can't believe you wanted me to change," Briar said as she walked down the stairs having changed out of those slacks that kept me distracted all morning. She changed into a cropped sweater and jeans that sat high on her waist.

I smiled when she stopped in front of me, my eyes looking over her freckles and the new septum ring she had in. A golden bee.

"Excited?" I asked.

She rolled her eyes, but they lacked their usual sass. "For going on a mystery date? Sure, if it makes you feel better then yes, Hot Shot, I'm excited."

I followed her to the car and moved to open her door. Briar's cheeks flushed before she got in. Soon after we took off, my hands tapped on the steering wheel as I drove, waiting for Briar to say something. It wasn't until we parked at the aquarium that she finally looked at me, her mouth open.

"This is our date?" she asked, smiling.

"Yeah. I called last week and they said this time of day usually isn't too busy. So hopefully we'll be able to have fun without the crowds. Do you like it?" I asked, suddenly nervous again.

She smiled. "Yes! I've never been to one, but you need to remember that this is so people can take pictures and gossip about you. Keep your hands to yourself so things don't, uh, happen."

I leaned in, taking in that sweet coconut smell, I couldn't help but grin. "Things like what?"

Her cheeks turned red but she held my gaze. "Things that will make you think there's a chance I'll end up in your bed again."

"I didn't realize taking a beautiful woman to get ice cream and an aquarium would get me laid. Maybe I should take notes while we're here. Would you be willing to fill out a survey when we're done? For science of course," I said with a click of my tongue.

Briar smacked my chest, the ring she wore on her

pointer finger dug into my skin. "You're not getting feedback or anything from me. Got it?" She was quiet for a moment as she bit her lip. "Did you actually ask for surveys though? Did anyone fill them out?"

I made a point to count my fingers and watched as her cheeks flushed and her expression morphed into a cute scowl. "At least ten. There were plenty others of course, but by the time we were done they were more occupied with learning how to walk than filling out the form."

"If you were the reason they couldn't walk then they sure are missing out on a majority of the male population. It wasn't anything to write home about."

I dropped my hand as I stared down at her. "Are you saying I'm not a good lay?"

She bit the inside of her cheek, as if to hide a smile, and shifted her gaze to look somewhere behind me. "You said it, not me." Briar brushed past me and opened the door. "Come on, I want ice cream."

This woman was trying to get under my skin, we *both* knew I wasn't lacking in *any* department. I just needed her to admit it to my face.

If that was possible.

We got ice cream, and to my surprise, Briar got a plain vanilla cone. No sprinkles or sauce to make it taste better, but I kept those comments to myself. Instead, I was entranced with the way she licked the ice cream up the side of the cone. Memories of our morning together made my pants tight, and I had to force my eyes elsewhere.

"This ice cream sucks. I've never had any that melted this fast," she said.

I shrugged, determined to be on my best behavior. "I think it's cause you're a slow eater."

"Don't blame me for this. We can't all eat our *frozen*

desserts in three bites. Seriously, how did you not get a brain freeze? I got one just watching you."

"When you have a lot of siblings you learn to eat fast. Because if you don't, there's a very good chance someone else will take it."

Briar shook her head. "That sounds horrible."

I laughed and leaned back in my seat. The ice cream shop was right inside of the aquarium, and there wasn't a line at the ticket booth so there was no rush for her to finish eating. "It did suck, yeah. But in a way it was kind of fun, beating the shit out of your brothers for the last cinnamon roll on a Sunday morning really solidifies the sibling bond."

"Does it really?" she asked with genuine curiosity.

"Yeah, and honestly growing up as one of six it was a lot of fun. I know not everyone has that experience, it's a lot to manage and it gets expensive. But my parents did their best and as far as I can tell none of my siblings feel any resentment. We all get together at least once a year for the holidays, and I know my brothers go see them once a month because they all live a lot closer. It makes me excited to have that one day."

Kids were a sensitive topic for some, and I wasn't sure how Briar felt about the whole thing. Hell, I still wasn't even sure how I wanted to navigate that with my current lifestyle, but I knew I wanted it. Briar nodded, licking absentmindedly as she stared into space. She was being too provocative without even knowing, and I mentally cursed myself for getting worked up over an ice cream cone.

"That would be really fun to experience. Being an only child I've always wondered what that would be like."

"So you want kids?"

"One day. I'm too young right now to want to commit myself to a family and kids. I want to explore the world and get to know myself more before I'm ready for all of that."

Images flickered in my mind; Briar and I exploring castles in Europe, Briar and I on a safari tour, Briar and I —us, together.

Briar finished her ice cream and when we walked toward the entrance I reached down and grabbed her hand, linking our fingers together. After we were handed our tickets and two wristbands to feed the stingrays, we headed toward the two escalators that led up to the first set of exhibits. It was then Briar tried to pry her hand away, but I held firm.

"This is a date you know," I said.

"Yeah but, there aren't enough people for it to matter. Right? I don't see anyone ready to snap a photo." For the first time since the night we left the wedding, she sounded nervous.

I placed my hand on her lower back and directed her to a quiet corner, with her back facing the wall and mine facing the crowd behind us. I interlocked our fingers again, my brows furrowed as I tried to keep her eyes on mine.

"Listen Clover, if you *really* don't want to hold hands then just tell me. I'm a big boy, I will respect your decision."

She blinked those pretty blue eyes, her shoulders sagged. "It's fine. I'm sorry, it's been a while since I've done any of this stuff. Dating, holding hands, all that stuff. That doesn't give you a reason to get carried away, okay? Hand holding isn't a gateway to sex got it?" Briar said with a pointed look.

I leaned down until my nose rested above her ear. "Funny. I wasn't even thinking about sex. What a dirty mind you have, pretty girl."

She made a choking noise, but I paid her no mind as I dragged her toward the first set of tanks. "Now let's go, I want to see all the funny looking fish and make fun of them before someone's mom makes a comment about how I speak around her kids."

Briar let out a giggle as I pulled her through the crowd to the other exhibits. Everything was blue and there were glass walls on either side of us as we walked. Fish with vibrant colors swam above our heads and Briar had to stop every few feet to point out one that was ugly, incredibly pretty, or one she knew a random fact about. I, on the other hand, focused on the large fish at the bottom of the tanks and wondered why fish needed teeth.

I thought all fish were the same, that they opened their mouths and swallowed their prey whole. Briar stood in front of me, watching a family of clown fish swim around and I-I couldn't help myself. I walked up behind her and wrapped my arms around her waist, my head rested on the top of her head. Her body stiffened for a split second, and if I hadn't been waiting for a reaction I would have missed it. My hands snaked down to her hips and I turned her around to face me.

"You know, you can tell me if you're uncomfortable with something."

"I know," she said, her voice breathless. Briar turned back around and grabbed my arms, placing them back on her waist where they originally were. "This doesn't mean anything though. Physical touch is a simple, bodily need."

I drew small circles with my thumbs and placed a kiss on the top of her head. "You don't need to tell me twice."

It sucked that we were leaving the next day. The team was traveling to the East Coast for two weeks, one of our longest road trips of the season, and part of me wanted to ask Briar to tag along. But that was because I wanted more. I needed to know what made her laugh, made her cry, and ask if she liked my pancakes or ate them because she didn't want me to feel bad. This date was a turning point, I could feel it. I hadn't let go of my belief that commitment wasn't for me, but something shifted inside me anytime Briar smiled at me and I figured we might as well make the most out of our fake relationship.

I pulled away first and grabbed her hand, taking in the smoothness of her skin as I dragged her toward the next exhibit.

This wasn't real. I had to remind myself of that.

briar

I really wished I knew how to cook, and that Scottie was a *snack household* kind of guy. Because all of these ingredients weren't going to do me any good. There were tortillas, bread, breadcrumbs, and various flours and sauces in the pantry. The fridge held condiments and cheeses, some of which I couldn't pronounce.

The only thing I could make without starting a fire was a cheese quesadilla, and only because I could stick that sucker in the microwave.

So I watched as my food went round and round on the glass plate, the hum of the microwave filling the emptiness of the kitchen. It was weird, being here alone, I'd gotten so used to Scottie's company that I didn't realize how isolated I was before I moved in.

I needed more friends.

It'd only been four days since he left with the team, and I found myself thinking of one thing and one thing only; how much Scottie surprised me. For a man who didn't do commitment, he was taking his job as a boyfriend very seriously. The microwave beeped and as I took out my food, staring at the cheese oozing out of the sides, I realized I couldn't rely on my roommate to do all the cooking. No matter how nice he looked over the stove, the concentration on his face as he chopped vegetables, how the veins in his hands—

No. I was going to learn how to cook.

I shoved the quesadilla in my mouth and started searching the kitchen for some kind of cookbook, because surely he had one. Right? Wasn't that a kitchen staple—a cookbook you bought years ago and then set on the counter, forever forgotten because you could find better options on your phone?

It made sense in my head, and I was shocked to find a very well-loved cookbook on the bottom shelf in the pantry. The edges of the pages were thin, showing just how many times the pages had been turned in search of delicious meals.

I wondered how many of these dishes Scottie had made over the years, which ones he favored and which ones he didn't like. After some flipping, I found a recipe that looked easy enough—a garlic and herb chicken with a side of potatoes.

I grabbed a scratch piece of paper and wrote down the ingredients as I tore into my food. I wasn't going to cook tonight, but when he got back I'd cook for him. Show off my cooking skills and prove to him that I could work my way around the kitchen. Not that he ever mentioned my lack of using the stove, or complained when I asked to steal some of the extra food he made.

Once my list was written down, I folded the paper and placed it under the fruit bowl where I wouldn't forget it. I then started to clean up my small mess and jumped a bit when the doorbell rang as I put a sheet of cookies into the oven.

No I couldn't cook, but that didn't stop me from following the instructions on the cookie dough packaging and making my late night, sweet treats.

When I opened the door, I was greeted by Basil, and a blonde woman with stunning curls next to her. I looked between them before smiling at Basil. "Hey! Uh, what's up?" I asked.

"We figured you might be as bored as we are since the guys are gone. Can we come in? You can say no, but Hollis might pressure you into changing your answer," Basil said with a kind smile.

"I will not!" Hollis said, stomping her foot. "If she doesn't want us over because we're intruding then I'm going to respect that. Gosh, you and Townes think I barge into people's homes for fun."

I couldn't help but laugh and move my body to the side. "Come on in, the place is a little too quiet for my liking."

Basil walked in first and Hollis stopped next to me. "I know this is a weird way to meet new friends, but I'm Hollis. You knew that, and you need to know I'm not super overbearing."

The more I looked at her the more familiar she seemed, and it dawned on me. She was the woman next to the big, tattooed guy—Townes if my memory served correct—when I did the walk of shame down the stairs at the Airbnb.

My cheeks heated and I did my best to seem unphased. "Nice to officially meet you," I said.

She smiled, and I had a feeling she knew why I was suddenly nervous. Hollis turned and we walked into the kitchen where Basil was unloading a gigantic bag I missed earlier.

"I know we came over unannounced so we brought snacks, and drinks, *and* a few games," she said as she set everything on the counter.

I picked up the hot pink box and read the rules on the back before setting it back down. "We can *not* play this. I mean, you two can cause you're married, but I can't do that to Scottie."

The game was a fun take on truth or dare, but it was spicy and required you to text your crush or partner whatever the card you picked said.

Basil grabbed it and scowled at her friend. "I told you to leave this at your place!"

Hollis shrugged. "Hey what's the point of a girls' night if we don't have at least a little bit of fun. Besides it's more for you two than me, Townes isn't the one traveling."

That was right, her husband had retired at the end of last season.

"It's fine Basil. It might be fun," I said, dragging my palms against my pajama pants. I didn't want to ruin anyone's fun, and besides the idea of sending dirty text messages to Scottie excited me. If he was able to flirt with me, then who said I couldn't do it back? It was great practice and would only make us seem more in love. A few pictures had circulated online from our date at the aquarium, and we seemed normal. Like two people who were enjoying their time together, but I knew it wasn't enough. The media was looking for one of those pictures that makes women want to say, *"aw, I wished someone looked at me like that."*

I reached for the pile of snacks on the counter. "What do you guys want to do first? The game? A movie maybe?"

Hollis and Basil looked at each other, sharing a coy smile before Hollis grabbed a drink. "Well I for one want to hear all about this dating thing you're doing. Basil hasn't told me much, and Townes isn't nosey enough to ask Case or Scottie anything. So spill."

I chuckled and moved toward the couch. The girls followed after, and we all settled into the plush fabric. I snacked on a few pieces of candy as I scrolled to find a movie to throw on. "If I'm being honest, it's going better than I expected."

Hollis squealed and Basil took a sip of her wine.

"Better how?" Hollis asked.

With the movie playing, I pulled my legs up and tucked them into my chest. "Better like I don't have to worry about anything going wrong. I knew his reputation going into this, but he hasn't done anything to make me doubt his intentions."

Despite my reassurances about it being okay if he decided to sleep with women while he was gone, he was adamant about not doing so. He never said it was for fear of ruining the illusion of us being together, in fact he never gave me a reason. I assumed it was because he was more worried about letting my dad down; it was the only thing that made sense.

"I'm glad he's being nice, not that I had any doubts he'd be anything but a gentleman," Hollis said, taking a large sip of her wine. "Now I need to ask you something important."

Basil and I looked at her when her tone went serious. I cleared my throat and shifted until my body was facing hers on the couch. "Okay, go for it."

"How was the sex?" she asked.

Basil choked on her wine and my jaw went slack. Hollis smiled and waited for an answer.

"You can't just ask things like that Hol!" Basil reached over and pinched Hollis's leg.

"Hey, you can't tell me you've never been curious!" Hollis stood on the couch and stepped over Basil, who sat at my side with a smirk.

"She barely knows us! What makes you think she's going to tell us about her sex life with our friend?" Basil tried to hide her smile behind her wine glass as she leaned forward.

"I've seen her do the walk of shame, I think that makes us close enough to talk about these things," Hollis said, laying her head on my shoulder.

The laugh that escaped me wasn't intentional, but I couldn't keep it down. It had been so long since I had friends like this. When Maverick and I were together, a lot of my old friendships slowly fell to the wayside. I never got an answer from any of them as to why we stopped talking. It sucked, and I was grateful Danny stayed by my side.

"She's right, Basil," I said between laughs. "Seeing someone walk of shame out of their friend's house entitles them to details."

"Oh my gosh," Basil said, shaking her head while Hollis lifted her head to grin.

"All I'll say is it was amazing."

"That's all you're giving us?" Hollis asked with a pout.

I laughed and looked at her. "Unless you're willing to tell me about your sex life, then yes, that's all you're getting."

"Well—" Hollis started before Basil threw a pillow at her.

We erupted into another fit of giggles before settling into a comfortable conversation getting to know each other. Hollis told me all about how she and Townes met, then Basil told me about her and Case. By the time we were done talking we'd gone through one of the bottles of wine Basil brought, and Hollis had turned on the game. The guys were playing Toronto tonight, and as much as I wanted to ask them to change the channel, I couldn't do it.

I tried to only watch the games when I was going to write a piece about it; I didn't watch for pleasure often. Not because I didn't like the game but because I always seemed to watch Scottie and missed everything going on.

I was filling my glass with more wine and my bowl with more snacks before the game officially began when my phone vibrated on the counter.

SCOTTIE

Are you going to watch our game?

ME

Wasn't planning on it.

Then you won't be able to imagine how good I look under my jersey when I'm skating. Here. This should help. see attachment

My eyes were glued to the screen. Scottie sent a mirror selfie—he was wearing full gear but had lifted his jersey and was biting the fabric. The lean muscles of his stomach were exposed, and my fingers ached to feel his skin against mine again.

I cleared my throat and looked around, as if I was going to get caught drooling over him.

I stared at that message a few minutes too long before I sent another one.

scottie

We won our last game and we were headed home the next day. As I walked toward the media room, I kept my eyes on that one text Briar sent me a week ago.

CLOVER

Good luck Hot Shot

I hadn't expected the four words to have such an impact on me, especially since I'd heard them before from previous hookups. They still tried to text me every now and again, but all those messages were going unread. I wasn't even sure if I wanted to reach out to any of them when Briar and I were done with this facade we were putting on.

The postgame interviews lasted about thirty minutes, and I would be a liar if I said I wasn't bummed that Briar hadn't texted me. Would I look too clingy if I texted her first again? Over the past week and a half, I'd been the one to initiate conversation, not that I minded since she always responded. It would be worse if she didn't and I was messaging her like an old person who called their grandchildren for help with their computer password.

Or... shit. *Was* I being an old person and hadn't realized it yet?

"Hey dude!" Riley threw his arm over my shoulder as we headed toward the team bus. "Are you coming out with us tonight?"

I shook my head and adjusted the strap on my shoulder. "Nah man, I'm pretty tired."

He dropped his arm and raised a brow. "You've been tired this whole trip! Come on, just one drink? I miss going out with you."

Riley wasn't usually one to pout but it was hard to deny him when his reasoning was solid. We used to wingman each other before Briar and I wondered how much Riley had been striking out without me at his side.

I followed him onto the bus and smiled at him when we sat down. "I can't promise more than one beer."

———

This party is boringggggg with a capital B.
Wish you were here.

CLOVER

Bet you say that to all of your hookups.

Only the prettiest ones.

......

idk how I feel being compared to other
people you've had in your bed.

Would you be shocked to know that I
don't bring people into my bed?

So where do you do it?

Usually the guest room. They don't know
the difference.

Why? I'm assuming your bed would be
more comfortable.

Are you that curious? If so I can help you
test your little theory.

I don't get flustered anymore, so you can
stop flirting with me.

For some reason I don't believe you,
besides flirting with you is fun.

I put my phone face down and chugged the rest of my
beer. In the past when I picked up women at bars or
parties, I'd take them to a nice hotel or their place. My
house was at the bottom of my list of options, but when
alcohol clouded my judgement or I was being rubbed
through my jeans, I picked it for convenience. But no, I
hadn't ever had anyone sleep in my bed.

It was a recipe for disaster because fucking led to
sleeping, which led to cuddling—which was only acceptable outside of my home. I couldn't emotionally invest
myself into someone when we were sharing a space with
an unknown thread count. My bed however, intimacy in

that thing had the potential of leading me to want to put a fat ring on someone's finger.

So why did I basically tell Briar she was welcome in my bed if that's what she wanted?

I ordered another beer, making my drink count three.

"You look like you could use some cheering up," Riley said as he placed another beer on the table. "I spy with my little eye a brunette who can't stop looking at you."

He pointed toward a woman who sat a few tables down, and he was right, she was pretty. But she wasn't Briar.

Her hair fell in loose curls over her top that threatened to snap under the pressure of her boobs. They were massive. I met her gaze, and she giggled at her friends before giving me a small flirty wave. I nodded curtly before looking back at Riley. My dick wasn't open for business, and I didn't know what had gotten into him to make him think it was.

"Don't do that, set me up. I'm off the market," I said.

Case looked up from his phone and scowled at Riley. "Yeah. You know he's got that thing with Briar. Why are you acting like he's single?"

Riley held up his hands, his expression turned stricken. "I didn't know what the deal was with that. Honest. Scottie told me he and Briar were a thing for the press, but knowing him, I assumed they had a deal when it came to seeing other people." He faced me, lowering his hands and tilting his head. "I'm sorry Scottie, really."

I waved him off. "I'd be lying if we hadn't had that conversation. But no, I'm off the market until this thing blows over."

I should be looking forward to it, going back to how my life was before that pretty redhead entered it. Living a life without commitment to anyone but myself and the team was easy. So why was I feeling a pull to commit to something else? It wasn't good for my psyche—I needed to spread my ginger wings and get my dick wet.

Soon. Preferably with Briar under me, or on top of me. I'd take either.

Wait. Fuck, no. Down Scottie.

"Hey Riley, do you mind getting another round? Take your time too, there's a blonde over there who looks nervous to come and talk to you," Case said as he kept his eyes on me.

Riley ran a hand through his hair before walking off, leaving me and Case alone.

"What's going on? You're being weird," he said.

"I'm not being weird? You're being weird assuming things about me," I said, looking at my phone in case I missed a text message.

Case leaned forward, pushing his drink to the side before folding his hands together. "You and I both know that you're a sensitive guy. Maybe not as much as Townes but you're up there. What's going on with you and Briar?"

"Why does anything have to be going on?" I asked.

"Do you think I'm oblivious? You know, you make a big deal of being so intuitive of the people in your life, yet you don't realize what's going on in yours."

I blinked and leaned forward, lowering my voice. "Are you drunk? Should I call Basil and have her call you so you can bug someone else?"

Case sighed and leaned back. "Look I'm not going to sugarcoat anything with you. You're acting differently and it's not a bad thing. I'm simply a concerned friend who wants to make sure you're doing okay."

I was acting different? No. Case was lying.

"Different how?" I asked, unable to control myself.

Case chuckled. "You're constantly smiling at your phone when Briar texts you, you haven't looked at another woman once, and I've seen your calendar. You've got dates planned out the ass for her."

"How do you know what's on my calendar?" I asked.

"Because you shared it with me and Townes a while ago and never bothered to revoke access. You've got a double date with Maverick when we get back?"

Damn, me and my impeccable planning abilities. I gave them access so when I organized game nights and outings we didn't have to blow up the group chat trying to coordinate with each other. Now that was coming back to bite me in the ass.

"You saw that?" I wasn't sure I actually put that in my phone.

Case nodded. "Yeah, Basil and Hollis went over earlier to see her. They talked and Briar mentioned it, and as a husband, I get special privileges to this kind of information. But anyway, the girls really like her and wanted me to tell you to invite her to game night."

Game night. How could I have forgotten? It was the perfect chance to formally introduce her to the guys. She'd love them.

Riley chose the worst moment to walk back to the table, drinks in hand and a woman at his side. "These are my teammates I was bragging about, Case"—he pointed to our captain—"and Scottie. He's a forward like me but I'm much more handsome," he joked.

The woman giggled and I shared a knowing look with Case before we stood. Case cleared his throat. "And we were just heading out, tired and all that. You two have fun though," Case said.

"What?" Riley asked, his expression falling.

"Have fun," I said as my hand landed on his shoulder.

Case and I left the bar and walked back to the hotel, which thankfully wasn't far. We went our separate ways at the elevator, mostly because I didn't feel like continuing our conversation at the bar. He had to be wrong, I wasn't acting different. I opened the door to my room, tossed off my shoes and stripped down to my underwear.

I was the same man I was almost two months ago before I met Briar. A man who wasn't into commitment, a man who didn't get excited over a text message, a man who—

My phone buzzed from its place on the charger and I dove for it.

If I'm being honest it's fun flirting with you too. Only a little though.

> I'm honored. And look, as much as I wish I could stay up and chit chat with the prettiest girl I've ever seen...I'm exhausted. Riley tried to play match maker after our game and then I talked with Case and...I'm tired.

Match maker? Why didn't you accept? You know I don't care so long as you're smart about it. Was the girl he wanted to pair you with not pretty enough for you? Boobs too small?

> It had nothing to do with her looks if you can believe it.

Oh? Then tell me...what kept you from taking her back to your room? I thought you were a player, Mr. Bachelor?

. . .

I mulled over an answer that was good enough, one that wouldn't send her running for the hills and fake breaking up with me when I got back. I wasn't going to beat around the bush.

My girlfriend.

briar

What on earth had I gotten myself into?

I had a fool proof plan for this year—I made a manifestation sheet every New Year's Eve—and it was all going to shit. I hadn't adopted a guinea pig, was nowhere near ready to run my first half marathon, and I found a grey hair. Which I didn't think was possible, did redheads even go grey before the age of eighty?

But of all the things that could have possibly happened this year—me finding an abandoned kitten behind a dumpster, winning the lottery, or finding out I was some lost royal princess—I ended up having a fake relationship.

My girlfriend.

That text message had taken up valuable mental space and it was becoming obvious something was wrong with me. If this were the sixteenth century, I'd be carted off to a mental asylum. During those times you were either married off at the ripe age of twelve or died a spinster at sixteen, and I surpassed both those milestones with nothing to show for it. All I had was my blog and my aversion to cooking.

My phone buzzed on the desk, pulling me back to the real world.

"Hello?" I asked as I shut my computer.

"Hi sweetie, are you busy?" Dad asked.

"Not anymore, why what's up?" I'd spent the past week working from home, going over tapes Dad had sent me and avoiding Scottie when I could. We went out for coffee three days ago and we made sure pictures were taken, but other than that interaction, I'd given him the cold shoulder.

His text made my heart soar and that was *not* good for me.

There were shouts on his end and I assumed practice had just let up, that or dad was putting them through an amazing workout that had them all shouting for joy. But that was me being hopeful, I knew better from watching Dad push athletes when I was in high school. At that time he worked at the local university and was doing his best to get a coaching job at the professional level, so he worked hard and did his best to produce the best athletes to be picked up all across the country.

"I've got some equipment to haul over to one of the colleges, but not enough time. Would you be willing to help take them for me? I'm stuck in meetings, otherwise I'd do it myself," he said.

I still had on my running clothes from this morning and didn't feel like shifting through the clean laundry on my bed so I grabbed my shoes and headed out.

"Can you text me the address? I'm leaving now."

"Of course, I'll see you in a bit," he said before hanging up.

The training center's parking lot was full when I arrived and had to park in the back, which sucked because my legs still felt like jelly from my run. Eight miles was no joke when you forgot to bring energy chews, and stretch—I'd wanted to be out of the house before Scottie left for practice to avoid his mushy goodbye.

See you later Clover! Don't miss me as much as I'll miss you, okay?

He'd follow up with a hug which I usually reciprocated for the simple fact that he smelled nice. The steady weight of his body around mine was just a tiny bonus that I only thought about when I was drifting off to sleep.

Did I mention I'd be put into an insane asylum if I was born in a different century?

When I got inside, I headed toward the athletic wing and stopped when I came to two glass doors. I stared at the little black box on the door and sighed before grabbing my phone. This would have been easier if Dad mentioned I needed a key card.

The phone rang once, twice, thr—

"Briar!" Scottie said as he opened the door. His hair was wet and he wore a huge smile on his flushed face. "What are you doing here?"

I stepped past him and continued down the hallway, making sure to keep my head on a swivel for any of his teammates. "My dad asked me to pick some stuff up for him while he's in a few meetings. Were you leaving or do you have some sort of sixth sense when it comes to my location?"

His smiled widened as he moved to the side, there was just enough space for me to walk past him, but not without my shoulder brushing against his chest. I kept moving forward only so he couldn't see how much I was trying to keep it together.

"I was on my way out actually, but running into you is even better," he said.

"Oh? Care to explain?"

We stopped at the equipment room and Scottie walked in first, only taking a couple steps before throwing out his arms. "Hey! Wasn't expecting to see you here, I thought you already left."

I peered around his lean, muscular frame and found Maverick with a smile of his own. It was kind, the one I was used to seeing but for some reason when his gaze darted to me, the hairs on my neck stood up. I smiled anyway, hoping to diffuse whatever tension he'd seemed to throw at me.

He turned toward us, a few pairs of skates in his hands. "I was going to go, but got these at the last minute. Did you guys need something?"

"Uh, my dad asked me to grab some equipment? The ones that are being donated or something?"

Maverick nodded. "Right." He turned toward two huge net bags filled with cones, skates, and other small equipment. "Here you go, everything should be in there, but if I missed something let me know. You still have my number right?"

I stepped forward to grab the bag, but Scottie beat me to it, his body suddenly tense. There was an awkward silence before I reached out and pinched the fabric of Scottie's athletic shirt. I tugged at the same time I nodded toward Maverick. "I might, if I need anything though I'll find you. Thanks for getting this stuff together."

He nodded. "Sounds good. We're still on for our double date, right?"

Shit. That was tonight. I'd forgotten an—

Scottie tucked his arm around my waist and grabbed

the bag from me. "Sorry man, I forgot that we had something planned. Can we reschedule?"

Maverick nodded, the movement tight. "No problem! It wasn't the best night anyway, so this works out for the best."

"Glad it worked out, sorry again. We'll see you later," Scottie said before directing us toward the hallway.

When we were in the parking lot and he dropped his hand, I looked at him. "Why did you cancel? We don't have anything planned."

I was more than grateful for the cancellation, but I needed to know why Scottie did it. He wasn't the kind of person to call things off, especially at the last minute. Earlier this week he promised to make a huge breakfast for us on his day off, and he followed through with it despite being sore from practice the previous day. That man could fall ill with some horrible disease making him bedridden and I knew he'd find a way to follow through on his word.

He shrugged as he tossed the bag into his car. "Didn't feel like going. I haven't seen you a whole lot this week and felt like spending time together. That okay with you?"

Was it a good idea to spend time with him when I was still deciphering his last text message? Did it have a double meaning or some hidden message that revealed he was growing feelings for me? If he was, would I be strong enough to put distance between us?

No.

I crossed my arms and stared up at him, taking in those red curls and freckled skin. "I guess I can clear my schedule."

He smiled and my heart soared. "Great. Are you hungry? Want to stop by the store when we're done?"

It was then my stomach growled, and I'd realized I'd been so caught up working I hadn't eaten a real meal all day. "Burgers?"

"We can do burgers. Maybe some homemade French fries too? My sister sent me a recipe for truffle fries that looked good, and I want to try it."

"That's kind of cute, you trying stuff she sends," I said as I looked at his car, then back to him. "Do you want to drive separately?"

He shook his head. "Let's drop your car off at the house first, then we'll drop this stuff off."

We were on the road soon enough and fought Denver traffic across town to the college. Scottie spent the ride with the music up, singing at the top of his lungs and trying to get me to do the same. At one point his hand landed on my thigh, he squeezed it as he looked at me and continued singing. It was cute.

When we reached the college, Scottie ran in himself to drop off the equipment while I waited in the car. I looked out the window as he came outside, smiling and walking with his head held high like he knew nothing could ruin his day. I turned the music up a little as he got back in the car and faced me.

"So groceries?"

I sighed, anxious about where this evening was headed. "Groceries."

———

"Ok, are you ready to get to work?" Scotty asked as he continued to place vegetables and cutting knives and other mysterious kitchen tools out in front of me. I stared at the vegetables and my hands went numb. What was I supposed to do with them? Just toss them in the oven?

What temperature did they need to be at, and wouldn't the potatoes explode? I saw a video on that once. How did I prevent that from happening?

To be fair I did try to get out of helping with dinner when he woke up from his nap, but Scottie insisted I help him. I took a healthy sip of my wine and looked at Scottie as false determination ran through me.

"I guess so. What should I do?" I could do this. I had a college degree, had some fancy award for my blog, courtesy of my loyal readers, and I knew how to put in a menstrual cup.

I could peel some potatoes.

Scottie smiled down at me, potato peeler in his hand, and I couldn't help but get caught up in the way he was looking at me. The blue in his eyes seemed lighter, his smile warmer. It reminded me of our first night together, how he looked at me when we danced in the snow. When he smiled at me the morning after before he went down to make breakfast. How often did he think about our night together?

Did he wish to be rid of me and this charade so he could experience that kind of pleasure again?

He placed the peeler in my hand, and I suddenly hated how stupidly handsome he was. "I'm putting you on potato duty. I'm thinking mashed? Or should they be roasted?"

Considering I didn't know how to make either, I just shrugged and grabbed a potato. I then stared at the counter as I tried to think of an excuse to walk away and Google how to use the peeler. It seemed straight forward but I couldn't risk cutting my fingers and severing a tendon or something.

When Scottie didn't walk away, I cleared my throat and took the potatoes to the sink. I could wash them while I came up with a game plan to cook them. He busied himself with cutting the chicken, and I was grateful he didn't look my way again.

I took my time peeling the potatoes, it wasn't as daunting as I thought it would be, but I was still slow to ensure I wouldn't cut myself.

"How's your book?" Scottie asked, holding up a paperback.

My cheeks went red when I saw what he was holding, but did my best to keep from jumping on him and taking the book from his grasp. Instead, I took a calming breath and continued the potatoes.

"It's good."

He leaned against the counter next to me and started flipping through the pages. "Just good? This is romance isn't it?"

I had to change the subject, there was no way in hell I was telling Scottie my current read was monster erotica I'd accidentally grabbed off the shelf. "Yeah, you know, it's the normal romance stuff that guys usually find boring." The knife slipped, and I pulled my hand away just in time.

He eyed me warily before he reached for a potato and started dicing it beside me, when I looked at him with a raised brow, he answered a question I didn't think to ask.

"I used to cook with my dad all the time," he said. "My mom has arthritis in her hands and has always had a hard time in the kitchen so my dad cooked most of the time growing up. I was always the first one to help him because my older brothers didn't like cooking and at the time my sisters were too young to take any interest."

I tried to imagine little Scottie in that scenario, surrounded by family, laughing with however many brothers and sisters he had, and I wondered what his childhood was like that made him into this happy go lucky goofy guy.

"Did you offer to cook or did your dad have to seek you out?" I asked as I grabbed another potato.

"Oh no, I always offered. My parents have paid for hockey since I was five years old and so I did things to show my gratitude. I helped cook, helped my mom around the house and I enjoyed it. My family was always here to support me, and I wanted to support them."

"That is really sweet," I said. Both of my parents were still in high school when they had me, and growing up they did their best to make sure I didn't feel like a burden. They didn't have support from their parents because they had me so young, but I honestly couldn't ever tell that they struggled. I thought everything was fine until my freshman year of high school, that's when they dropped the news they were getting a divorce.

That was a great way to start off high school.

"My parents never taught me to cook, if you can believe it." I chuckled. "We survived on takeout and oven dinners. My mom learned how to cook through one of her ex-husbands who was a chef, and I don't think my dad knows how to make anything more complex than spaghetti."

"I figured that was the case when you looked at the potato peeler like you were looking at a vibrator for the first time." Scottie smiled wide enough to make the corners of his eyes wrinkle.

I gasped and smacked his cheek. "That's not true! I totally didn't have that reaction to a vibrator."

"Oh you're telling me a potato peeler stumped you and not a vibrator?"

"Can you please stop saying that word?"

He laughed. "What? Vibrator? What's wrong about it? A lot of people—"

As he was talking, I continued cutting the potatoes, but I'd been so focused on the conversation I hadn't been paying attention to my hands. I was on my last potato when the knife went down at a weird angle. My finger stung as I grasped it in my free hand, dropping the knife on the floor.

"Ow, fuck."

Scottie was on me in a second while I kept my eyes closed, too scared to look at the damage. He pulled my hand away from my chest and began inspecting the cut through the blood.

So much blood. I was probably going to lose my finger if a doctor couldn't fix it.

There went my career.

"Here, sit down," Scottie said just before he hoisted me up onto the counter. He grabbed a first aid kit from under the sink and placed it beside me.

I had to talk, otherwise I was going to cry. "You're prepared."

He grabbed my hand and started cleaning my finger while I kept my eyes closed and focused on his gentle touches.

"Yeah, well, my old roommates were our team's goalie and his niece. First day living with me she cut her leg on a rock outside after falling down, so I learned quickly to keep this thing stocked."

Scottie continued working on my finger, taking great care to clean the wound and bandage it up. I didn't look at it the entire time, instead I focused on the furrow between his brows and the blues of his eyes. When he finally looked at me, with his hands on my legs and the softness returning to his face—I wanted to say something, but words eluded me. He stepped between my legs and held my injured hand to his chest.

"Are you okay?" His thumb brushed the back of my hand, and I had to control my breathing.

"Yes. Thank you."

He took a step back and stared at all the prepared food, then sighed. "I haven't started the burgers. Why don't you order a pizza while I clean this up."

"Are you sure? I don't want to waste food," I said, peeking over his shoulder to the groceries.

Scottie smiled. "It's fine. I care more about your company than what we eat. So, pizza?"

I nodded and hopped off the counter with butterflies in my stomach, careful to avoid bumping my finger against anything. "That sounds good, I can put a movie on too maybe? Unless you don't want to watch one?"

Scottie smiled. "A movie sounds great."

He took a step back and I wanted to stay in the kitchen and help him, but for some insane reason I couldn't contain the heavy feeling in my chest, the embarrassment of cutting myself, having him wrap my finger, enjoying the feeling of how close he was to me.

I reminded myself that inside this house we needed to keep our distance. To save the touches for when we were outside of the house. Otherwise, the feelings I had blooming for him would erupt into a field of wildflowers I'd never be able to control.

scottie

"Have you ever been to a charity event?" I asked with a raised brow.

Briar checked the pizza tracker again before letting out a sigh, she tucked her feet under her on the couch and shook her head. "I mean, in college I'd go to some student-run ones, but it wasn't ever anything super fancy."

"Okay but you kind of know what to expect? Suits and dresses no one can breathe in? Fancy whore durves that don't actually fill you up so you're forced to stop and get fast food on the way home?"

Briar's brows creased as she looked at me, a question in her eyes. "Did you just say whore durves?"

"Yeah?"

She laughed and I wondered for a minute if it was normal to like the sound as much as I did. "I can't tell if you're saying it like that on purpose or not, but it's hors d'oeuvres."

"I can't tell the difference if I'm being honest with you," I said with a shake of my head. "Anyway, can you dance?"

The doorbell rang and Briar jumped up to grab the pizza, but it took her longer than it should have to shut the door. Her voice carried into the living room and she sounded—anxious? I stood, groaning from the soreness of my body, and walked to the door. She was holding the two boxes of pizza she ordered, but the delivery guy—who appeared to be ten years too old for her—had a foot in the threshold and I saw red.

"Everything okay?" I asked as I walked up next to her, placing my hand on her waist. Briar physically relaxed under my touch, and I couldn't help but rub my thumb up and down, neither of us caring that I ended up touching her exposed skin between her shirt and the waistband of her pants.

The delivery guy visibly paled and removed his foot. "Sorry man, we were just talking."

"Mm. Well next time I catch you talking to my girlfriend with your foot in our house I'll break it," I said, ice coating every word before I slammed the door in his face. Then, I grabbed Briar's phone from her back pocket and turned it to her face.

"What are you doing?" she asked, following me into the kitchen.

"Figuring out what his name was so I can call and complain." When she didn't say anything I gave her a flat look. "No objections?"

She shrugged and placed the pizzas on the table. "Why would I? He made me uncomfortable and the situation is being handled. I'm not going to stop you just because I *should* feel uncomfortable about calling out bad behavior."

God she was amazing.

I nodded, then proceeded to call the pizza place while she got us plates and returned to the couch.

As it turned out, I wasn't the first to complain about our delivery driver and I was left very satisfied after the phone call. The man would most likely get fired, all I could do was hope his next job was away from customer service. Maybe he'd get a job at a landfill, it seemed very fitting for someone like him.

I settled next to Briar and grabbed her foot, my unanswered question burning in my throat. "So dancing. Do you have two left feet or two right ones?"

Her cheeks went red and she tried to kick me, but I held firm. "Since you weren't paying attention when I was naked, I have one of each and yes they're on their correct sides."

My thumb pressed into the arch of her foot, earning me a soft, suppressed groan.

I did it again because that sound had been haunting me for months. It was delicious, something I'd eat over and over again without getting tired of it. But this time she kept quiet, and I didn't want to push my luck. But because I'm me and I didn't like to keep my mouth shut, I smiled at her.

"I'm sorry. I was a little more focused on the rest of you when you were naked."

Redness took over her pretty features, almost drowning out her freckles and I couldn't help but stare. She shook her head and took a huge bite of her pizza before we plummeted into silence. It wasn't awkward or uncomfortable in any way, just two people content in each other's silence. When we were both done, I took her plate and set it back on the coffee table.

"Can I ask you something?"

"Go for it," she said as she tucked her legs beneath her.

I cleared my throat. "Why Maverick? I mean you said you guys dated in high school but he's kind of—"

"Kind of what?" Briar asked.

I had a hard time wrapping my brain around Briar and Maverick being together, and an even harder time understanding how she didn't see what a total dick he was. Sure they were both grown now, but I had a hunch that Maverick wasn't too different now than back then. He was too abrasive, and I wondered if Briar saw it, or if maybe I was too in my head about her ex-boyfriend.

Which seemed crazy since we weren't, well—

Briar was too good for him, and me, but that's not the point. She was disciplined in how she ran every morning like it was her job. She was kind when she offered to pay me back whenever she took one of my snacks from the kitchen. She woke up early to get work done before I left for practice and always made extra coffee so I'd have some when I woke up.

She cleared her throat. "You're not the first person to ask why I dated him you know. Danny was the first, and a few old friends asked too. If I'm being honest he wasn't the best person for me to be with. He wasn't the nicest." Briar shook her head as her voice wavered and it almost broke me. How could anyone treat anyone, especially her with anything but kindness.

A tired smile tugged at the corner of her mouth. "But that's in the past, tell me more about this charity. What organization are you raising money for?"

I wanted to ask for more information about Maverick, but I didn't want to push her.

"Um, I think it's for cancer research. Everyone on the team has been tasked with offering something of theirs for auction. Case is auctioning baking lessons with him, Riley is auctioning himself for a date," I said.

"What about you?" Briar asked without looking at me, instead choosing to focus on the bottom of her pants.

Why wouldn't she look at me? I loved when she did that.

"No idea yet. I was going to do the same thing as Riley, but that's not happening."

Her eyes widened slightly as she cocked her head to the side. "Why not?"

"Because we're fake together?"

"That doesn't mean you can't auction yourself for charity though. What are your other options? Giving away a signed jersey or something equally as lame? Honestly you might get more money if you auction off a date. Women love what they can't have, and I bet there's going to be a bunch of old ladies willing to fight over you."

There was tension in her voice I hadn't heard before, I leaned down with a smirk, already having an inkling into what she wasn't saying.

"You're not jealous are you?" I asked.

She sucked in a breath. "No. Why would I be?"

"I'm not sure, but you sounded like it."

"Trust me, if I was jealous, you'd know. But that's never going to happen because we are never going to happen. Once your public image or whatever is fixed, and I get a job with the network, we can separate and go about our lives like normal."

Normal. For some reason the thought of going back to how I lived before Briar didn't sit well with me. I'd grown fond of our little arrangement, getting to know her over coffee and hearing her laugh over my jokes at dinner. I wanted to keep her for a little longer.

I raised a brow. "So if I dance with a woman at the auction, you won't even pretend to be a jealous girlfriend?"

"Why would I get jealous?"

I snorted. "Clearly you haven't seen how I can be with other women."

"Well show me then," she said, her nostrils flaring in defiance.

She stood and walked around the corner, making sure to sway her hips and flip her loose hair over her shoulder so it cascaded down her back. Briar was only there for a minute before she came back, holding my gaze and smiling, but it was wrong—too wide. In that moment she wasn't Briar, she was every other woman I was used to interacting with at social events, well the ones who knew me anyway. When you surrounded yourself with other athletes—and everyone else who made your team successful; equipment managers, medical staff, nutritionists—you were bound to meet a lot of different people.

In some people's experience that would be the professionals; coaches, agents, and managers. However, in my experience I met all the women who liked to hang off athletes arms and look pretty for the cameras. I think that was what made it so easy to hook up with them, we shared the same goals—have a good time with someone you didn't have to see again.

Briar sauntered up to me and her hand hovered over my arm as she dragged it down. "Hey handsome. If memory serves me correctly, I won a dance with you."

My skin prickled under her invisible touch, a stark contrast to how it felt when I first touched her. I didn't understand it—the effect she had on me—but I knew I didn't like how she was pretending. Acting like all the other women I was used to. I wanted her to just be Briar.

"Don't do that," I said as my finger twitched when her hand reached my wrist. It didn't touch her, but if I wanted to I could. I kept my head down. "I don't like you pretending to be someone else."

"But isn't that how other women approach you? I'm just doing what they do," she said with curious eyes, meeting my lowered gaze.

I shook my head. "I don't want you approaching me like someone you're not. How does that help me be genuine when you're not doing the same?"

Briar stared at me for a moment and then nodded before she cleared her throat. "Okay take two." Her smile melted into the one I was familiar with, and I smiled as she looked up at me. "Care to dance? Or did I waste my money on someone with two left feet?"

"No no, your money hasn't gone to waste. My girl-friend is the one who can't dance, so if anything, your money was well spent."

Her brows creased together as I took one of her hands in mine and placed the other on my shoulder, my free hand settled on the dip of her waist.

"Girlfriend?" she asked.

I lowered my voice. "You don't really expect me to chat these women up like they have a chance right? I need to establish at the start that I'm off limits."

"But you're not, not really."

I lowered my head until my nose was in her hair. "Shh, let me play this out."

She chuckled, trying to cause a distraction from the goosebumps covering her skin. "I wish I could help, but I don't know what rich women talk about."

I pulled her closer and swayed side to side. "We don't need to talk about anything really."

So we didn't. We danced in the living room in silence; the only sound was our breaths which grew heavy as our bodies pressed closer together. Briar's front was completely against mine and I knew what I'd see if I looked into her eyes, because I was thinking the same thing.

I wanted her. There was something about her that drew me in, like she was the sun and I was a pathetic planet seeking her warmth. Hell, she could be any planet, in any solar system and I'd always ask for the privilege to be in her orbit.

I was horrible at keeping secrets, and not telling Briar about the expansion of warmth in my chest was going to eat away at me if I didn't do something about it soon. The answer was simple, either we stopped what we were doing, or I told her that if I kept being her fake boyfriend, then I'd have to make it the real deal soon enough.

Relationships might still scare the shit out of me, but if Briar was by my side I knew it would be okay.

Before I could tell her that though, she dropped her hand and tilted her head until we were eye to eye. "I think if you promise to tell every woman you dance with that you have a girlfriend, I won't get jealous, even if it's all for pretend's sake."

Briar stepped away and crossed her arms over her body as she walked backward toward the stairs. "Thanks for helping with my hand." She held up her bandaged finger. "I've got to get some interviews prepped and stuff. Text me when you leave in the morning?"

I nodded and smiled. "Of course. I'll see you later Clover."

She paused and dropped her arms, tilting her head she grinned. "See ya Hot Shot."

Then she was walking upstairs, leaving me with a stunning realization. I couldn't ever go back to how I lived my life before, not after knowing how Briar felt in my arms.

scottie

"Uno bitches," I said, throwing down my blue eight.

Townes grumbled and placed his cards on the table while Hollis sipped her beer. Case shook his head, pulling Basil further into his lap while she stared at the pile. She pinned me with a scowl, her hazel eyes growing darker either because of her inability to accept defeat or because she wasn't as good at this game as she initially claimed.

Either way it sucked to suck.

"You cheated," she said, pointing a finger at me.

I stuck out my tongue, not because I was a child, but because how *dare* she make such an accusation. "Nuh-uh. You just suck at card games."

Briar apparently decided at that moment that the orgasm I gave her meant nothing, she shoved her hand into my pocket and pulled out a slightly crumpled yellow two, her brows were creased as she flipped the card toward everyone.

"Yes he did."

"Whose team are you on anyway?" I asked, taking the card from her, our fingers brushing each other. A tingle encased my arm, and I tried to shove the feeling away. Sure, my body had been going haywire since our little dance in my living room, but it didn't mean anything. I was no-romantic-feelings Scottie Lancaster and nothing was going to make me *have* feelings. Briar's soft skin, coconut smell, pretty smile, blue eyes, and her—

Nope. Stop it.

Briar hid her grin with her cards and avoided making eye contact. "There's no teams in Uno. Everyone knows that," she said.

I reached for her chair and gripped the bottom before I yanked her toward me, our thighs pressed together and her breath hitched. Everyone was staring, but I didn't care as I leaned in to whisper in her ear. "It's common knowledge that you help the person who gets you off. Or did you really think those guys weren't conspiring against us?"

Briar's eyes flickered to the other couples, her cheeks a rose pink as she considered my words. I leaned back in my seat and crossed my arms. "Your turn, Townes."

"No no no, we're not moving past this so easily Lancaster. I think if you *cheat* you have to start with a full hand. Isn't that right Case?" he asked.

Our captain shook his head, and I placed my hand on my chest in shock. "You're agreeing with him? The guy who made you draw four?"

"I mean, he didn't cheat like *someone* at the table," he said with a shrug.

Game night was supposed to be fun; a time best friends could get together and bond over competitive screams and table flipping. It wasn't where people could gang up on one person because they slipped a card or two into their pockets.

Townes brought loaded dice out whenever we played Yahtzee—you didn't see me calling him out.

I needed to find a way to keep Briar on my side and to keep her from telling everyone when I made a card disappear. I brushed my thumb against her thigh and watched as goosebumps littered her skin. She was wearing her green pajama shorts—my favorite ones—they resembled boxers with how they hung from her waist, and I couldn't help from touching her. Not now when no one could see us under the table. Briar had been unusually touchy these past few weeks, coming up and giving me a hug, holding my hand while we watched movies. It was nice.

Townes raised a brow, and I cleared my throat, removing my hand from Briar and putting it on my thigh. "We've all cheated, are we really going to make a big deal of it now?"

"I've never cheated," Hollis said with a smile. She had two canines that sat forward, giving them a cute snaggled look.

Townes tried to cover his laugh with a cough, but he wasn't fooling anyone.

"Tell that to literally anyone who has ever played against you in monopoly," Basil said.

"Hey! You're supposed to cheat, everyone knows that."

"No you're not," Townes said, smiling at his wife. "I let you do it anyway though."

Hollis gasped. "You *let* me?"

"Mhm. And Hayley too. Neither of you are as slick as you think."

Case knocked on the table and raised a brow when he had everyone's attention. "Are we going to keep playing or move onto something else?"

Briar smiled. "Have you guys ever played Scene It? I have the Disney version upstairs in my closet."

We all looked at each other, and I could see the competitiveness in Case and Townes's eyes, it was the same look they had before stepping on the ice. I was only mildly surprised seeing it on Townes, considering he hadn't played with us since he retired last season.

I leaned in until I could see the goosebumps on her skin from my proximity. "I don't know how good of an idea that is, they might not look like it, but those two are huge Disney fans."

Hollis stood and patted Townes's shoulder. "Might as well get it Bri, cause these two aren't going to stop."

"Yeah, if we don't play it now, then they'll come busting through the door when Case and Scottie get back next week," Basil said, going to stand next to Hollis.

The guys were staring at each other, a silent conversation between them as their forgotten cards laid on the table.

Briar nodded and pushed away from the table. "Just make sure they don't kill each other while I go grab it."

While she was grabbing the game and I cleaned off the table, Hollis was finishing up our dishes from earlier and putting them in the dishwasher while everyone else was arranging the blankets and pillows on the couch. By the time I made it into the living room, they had converted the floor into a gigantic pallet.

Briar walked up behind me and before she could walk past me, I turned around and grabbed the game from her with a smile and a wink. Her lips parted and I was proud of the self- control I had to turn away and put the game into the DVD player.

Briar

Scottie was a big, muscular traitor.

He sat across from me on the huge makeshift pallet, and I wasn't opposed to having Townes as my partner, but I had a feeling Scottie paired up with Hollis to piss the guy off.

"Okay everyone shut up! The first question is about to play," Case said, putting a finger to his lips.

Everyone had their eyes glued to the screen, and it was Hollis who screamed the answer out after the question played out. *"Bambi!* The movie is *Bambi!"*

"Are they always like this?" I asked Townes.

Townes smirked. "Yes."

This was the first time I'd seen everyone together. Basil texted me last week to plan a game night, and according to her, two days later Scottie showed up at their house with a plate of sympathy pancakes. He was faking being upset that I'd been chosen as the new favorite friend, and that she went behind his back to make plans with me.

I thought it was hilarious, only because he coerced them both into handing over a few baggies of brownies. I wasn't going to complain about his behavior when it meant I got a few sweet treats out of it.

He faced me as Case continued onto the next question and raised a brow. "So you and Scottie huh?"

My cheeks heated and I had never been more grateful for the lights to be off. "Wh-what're you talking about?"

Townes gave me a flat look. "I'm talking about how obvious you two are. I thought you were dating for the press, when did it get serious?"

I scoffed and crossed my arms, Case and Scottie were in an argument across from us. "I have no idea what you're talking about. It's not serious, nothing is serious."

"You expect me to believe you don't have feelings for each other?"

Despite the fact I was sitting crisscross applesauce, all the blood in my body rushed to my feet and I felt woozy.

"Shit are you okay?" Townes asked, holding out a hand, as if he would catch me if I passed out.

I cleared my throat. "I'm fine it's ju—you"—I pointed a finger—"don't know what you're talking about."

He rolled his eyes and put his hand back to his side. "Yes I do."

"No you don't," I whispered.

Scottie didn't have feelings for me, and I didn't have any for him either. Friends could smile at each other and seek physical comfort from one another. Our relationship was completely platonic with no chance of romantic feelings ever coming to a head. That was what I'd told myself the past few weeks anyway. I couldn't pinpoint when I felt the need to be closer to him and I wasn't going to question it. I'd decided to go with the flow until I either crashed and burned or found the love of my life.

Scottie stood and threw his arms out to the television. "What do you *mean* you've never seen *Robin Hood*? How can you call yourself a true Disney fan if you haven't seen that classic?"

Basil shook her head. "I only watch the good movies, Scottie."

Scottie went on a tangent, and I couldn't help but

laugh at his enthusiasm. When my gaze drifted back to Townes, I caught him smirking, and I swiftly looked away.

Townes kept his voice low enough for just me to hear, not that anyone else would with how loud Case and Scottie were arguing. "He's a good guy, I hope you both know what you're doing."

I wasn't going to tell him that we didn't, not really. I was fighting the small flicker of feelings that decided my chest was the perfect place to call home. They couldn't call my body home, I wouldn't let them. Because at the end of the day, neither of us were looking for anything more than we were.

Townes and I didn't answer very many questions the rest of the game, mostly because neither of us wanted to face the wrath of our friends. At one point Scottie held back Hollis when she tried to tackle Case to keep him from shouting out an answer. I made a mental note to not play this game with them ever again.

When Case and Basil won, Scottie sulked and didn't offer much enthusiasm when everyone announced they were leaving for the night. It wasn't until I shut the front door and re-entered the kitchen that Scottie stood, his head hung low as he made his way toward me. One of his fingers twitched as his hands dangled at his side, there was a faint pink across his cheeks.

"I need a hug. I don't take losing very well," he said, his arms lifting toward me.

I smiled before walking into his arms, and I felt him relax as he caged me to his chest. It took a lot of effort to not shove my nose into his cotton shirt, if only to soak him in more.

His thumb rubbed the spot between my shoulder blades, but the gentle movement was contradicted by how tense his body was. I placed my hands on his waist and went to move away, but he stopped me.

"Just another minute, I like being here," he said.

I shook my head and pulled back. "Come on, you've got a big travel day tomorrow."

He squeezed me tighter to him, and I was too weak to fight back. Because fight as I might, I was in a losing battle with my heart. I liked being this close to him and for the first time since that meeting with my dad, I was dreading when we'd come to an end and go our separate ways.

scottie

I knew throwing a punch was a bad idea, but when the opposing teams defense body slammed into Case—leaving him gasping for breath—I lost it. My nose was bloody and my knuckles hurt, but not as bad as the dude's face did. We were in the last period with five minutes left on the clock, and I couldn't help but feel like the hit was intentional.

They got rid of our team's best center and left us scrambling when we're tied so they had a better chance at scoring.

What dicks.

Case had thankfully gotten up, but was taken to get checked out by the medical staff. I insisted on following, but Coach said I was *fine* and sat me on the bench. The referee, much to everyone's relief, called a minor penalty in light of the circumstances. But when my two minutes were up, Coach had me sit out the rest of the game. A decision he didn't give me any insight into, which didn't do anything for my mood. I was torn between being anxious he had found out I lied to him about Briar, and angry he wasn't letting me just finish the game on the ice.

Helpless to do anything, I watched the rest of the game with crossed arms and my bad mood worsened when we lost. I internally blamed Coach for pulling me, but I wasn't going to stick around to hash it out with him. When the final buzzer rang, I wasted no time heading to find Case, ignoring the boos from the opposing team's fans for punching their best defenseman.

But honestly, they could suck my left nut sack for all I cared, these past two weeks had been shit. We had barely scraped by during every single one of our games, and Case was our third teammate who ended up needing medical care. To top it all off, Maverick was being difficult anytime I needed something from him, being short tempered. I chalked up the bad behavior to canceling our double date at the last minute. Which was fair, but still. We had since rescheduled so I didn't know what was up his butt

I couldn't wait to get home. I missed Briar, and honestly, I was looking forward to parading her around in front of her ex during our date, and I wasn't just saying that because I wanted an excuse to put my hands on her body.

Or so I told myself.

When I walked in the medical room, Basil was already at Case's side, grasping his hand and pushing hair out of his face. She'd taken some time off from coaching her little league team to travel with us these past couple weeks, and Case couldn't have been happier. However, to my knowledge, this was the first time she'd seen him get hurt—at least this bad.

"I said I'm fine, sunshine, even Betty said so," Case said, rubbing Basil's back as she hung onto him.

An older woman standing next to him turned, her brunette hair was tied into a low pony. Her jaw hung open as she scolded him. "You have a *concussion.* You're lucky he didn't send you to the hospital with how hard you got hit."

Case chuckled and nuzzled his nose into Basil's hair. "See? Fine."

From the tension in Basil's body I could tell she wasn't having it, she kept her voice low as she spoke to him. I gave them their moment before walking over to them and nudging his knee.

"Don't scare us like that man," I said.

Case raised a brow, and Basil pulled away, smacking him lightly in the chest. "Listen to the ginger if you're not going to listen to me."

"I think you scared more people with how hard you hit that guy. I'm surprised I'm the only one back here," Case said, grabbing Basil to keep her from smacking him again.

I didn't make it a habit of picking fights during games, but I would do it for any of my teammates. Or friends. When I was younger, I was tasked with protecting my little sisters after our brothers went off to college, so you could say old habits die hard.

"It looked worse than it was," I said with a shrug. "Anyway, I just wanted to make sure you were good before I headed out. How long until you can play again?"

Betty turned to us, that scowl still on her face. "We will reevaluate in a week and go from there."

"Sounds like a plan, text me if you guys need anything okay?"

Basil and Case nodded before I turned and walked

back to the locker room for a quick shower. Once I was clean, I met Riley hanging out in the parking lot, typing away on his phone as I walked up to him.

"What are you still doing here?" I asked, slinging my duffle over my shoulder. We were heading home tomorrow afternoon and I knew most of the team had already gone back to the hotel for a good night's rest because we had all experienced flying while hungover and it was *not* fun.

Riley shrugged. "I found a dive bar not too far from here and was going to check it out, I was waiting to see if you wanted to come?"

I shook my head and gripped the strap of my bag tighter and Riley shrugged. "Alright man, I'll catch you later then."

I headed back to the hotel, more than grateful it wasn't far from the arena, and soon enough I was back in my large, plush hotel bed. My head hit the pillow at the same time my phone vibrated on the nightstand.

It was a picture of Briar wearing a sea blue dress. The straps crossed over the back of her neck, leaving her shoulders completely bare. It looked satin, like the dress she wore to the wedding, but this one—holy Jesus it hugged her better than air against bare skin. My eyes traced every tiny curve I could see in the photo, and I started to wonder how easily it came off, if there was a zipper, or if that small strip of fabric was the only thing holding it up.

CLOVER

I hope this is charity event approved?

It's not actually.

Why not? I thought it looked really nice!

Oh trust me it does.

Then what's the issue?

I can see your boobs clear as day.

….You're saying it's not appropriate
because you can see the outline of my
boobs? That's not a valid reason because
guess what, Hot Shot, my boobs are
outlined in EVERYTHING.

Well guess we need to skip out then. Such
is life.

Actually. There might be something I
could wear…

Briar sent another picture.

I stared at my phone contemplating my options which were; open it and potentially fantasize about my fake girlfriend to help my blue balls situation, or be a good athlete and do what my coach asked and keep an eye on his daughter.

I was positive this wasn't what he meant.

To open the picture or not—I tried to rationalize why this conversation was happening in the first place. We were flirting—I knew it when I saw it, hell I was an expert at it—so why was I so caught off guard? She didn't even like me like that.

Right? I'd spent the last month convincing myself my growing feelings were one-sided. Was I wrong?

I mean, in the short time since we'd met, I had never felt romantic feelings from Briar even though we felt connected. Maybe it was because we slept together, I remembered my sister talking about soul ties and stuff, or maybe it was because of some other cosmic force linking us. Either way, I wasn't going to complain. After a long moment I came to the realization that I was a fragile man with malleable morals, I opened the picture—and I stopped breathing.

Briar was sitting in front of the floor-length mirror she had in her room, wearing one of my jerseys. The fabric was hitched over her hips on either side, leaving the curve of her sides on full display as the jersey drowned out the rest of her frame. She wore her hair down her back and a hat—another item she stole from my room. The picture shouldn't have made me hard, her body was still hidden, but knowing what was underneath and not being able to see it—that was the part that killed me.

Clover girl…

Thought this was acceptable because you can't see my boobs. Was I wrong?

It's not your boobs that are the problem…

Oh silly me. They were the only thing you commented on so I didn't think to worry about anything else. Anyway I think I like this more. I'm keeping it.

You can't steal my clothes…you're too pretty and you're a tease.

Then I guess you'll have to come take it
back, fair warning though I'm not going to
give it up easily. It smells good.

.…

What are you doing?

…

What ever do you mean?

The flirting. Is this part of the boyfriend
thing? Need proof that we sext if anyone
goes through your phone? Because I'm
more than willing to do this for you.

Honest?

Wouldn't ask for anything less…

I accidentally ate some chocolate I found
in your room (don't worry I'll pay you
back) and funny enough….it's that sex
chocolate.

YOU ATE SEX CHOCOLATE????

Yes. I was putting some laundry away and
noticed it on the dresser, so I took some.
But if you're going to make a big deal of it
then I'll stop texting you and take care of
it on my own.

Wait who said I didn't want to help?

I wondered what she was doing right now, was she
dragging her hand over her body, over my jersey? Was her
body getting hot and aching to get fucked? I hadn't gone

this long without sex since I joined the team, but having Briar send me pictures and admit to taking aphrodisiac chocolate wasn't helping to keep my boner at bay.

My pants grew tight and I couldn't help but roll my hips into the mattress. Imagining the sounds Briar made when I kissed her body, when she came on my tongue. My hips moved faster, trying to get relief from the heat that pooled in my stomach. I wouldn't touch myself, not when she was off limits.

She didn't respond again, and I was too pent up thinking of her lips, her gasps, to care. I started moving my hips again, my hands flexing as I fought the urge to relieve myself of the building pressure in my cock. This wasn't right. She was a one-time thing like all the others—so why couldn't I get her out of my head.

I groaned and continued grinding my hips into the bed, seeking out the friction I so desperately needed. My fingers gripped the pillow and I turned my face toward it as my hips picked up speed. The heat spreading through my body and the slight ringing of my ears distracted me from the name coming from my mouth.

"Clover."

"Clover."

"Ah fuck. Briar."

A shudder ripped through me as I came in my pants, and I had to take a minute to gather myself before grabbing my phone. Kneeling on the bed, I didn't bother cleaning myself up before taking a picture from my point of view. My stomach on display, a dark spot on my grey pants, and a wet spot on the sheets. I didn't send her the picture—though I wanted too. Instead, I put my phone on the charger, closed my eyes, and did my best to not think about the pretty redhead as I drifted off to sleep.

briar

Never. Eat. Sex. Chocolate.

The mantra had been on repeat ever since the text messages Scottie and I exchanged last night. I'd been trying my best to convince myself it really wasn't worth it, hooking up with him again but *damn*—he called me pretty and I was a sucker for sweet words.

I huffed and tucked my hair behind my ears, flipping my phone over again as I tried to get my thoughts together. I was supposed to be finishing up another piece on the Peaks, a collection of interviews I'd done and a piece on their latest loss. It sucked, but it was my job. Instead of working though, I'd been distracted by the inevitable text Scottie would send me after his plane landed.

My phone vibrated and I grabbed it a bit too eagerly, which earned me a snort from my bed. I turned and rolled my eyes at the brows Danny was wiggling in my direction.

"You're excited. Who's texting you?" he asked with a shit eating grin.

I hadn't told him about last night, how my consumption of aphrodisiac chocolate—something that I wasn't even sure was legal—led me to flirt with Scottie. It was something I was still coming to terms with; had I just been lonely? Or was it because there was something about Scottie I couldn't run away from no matter how hard I tried to convince myself it was the best thing to do?

"Is it your hottie of a roommate?" Danny asked, coming to stand behind me, bracing his hands on my chair.

I rolled my eyes and turned my phone over again before looking back at Danny. "So what if it is? I'm expecting a text from him, it's not like I'm grabbing my phone out of desperation or anything."

Danny shrugged and grabbed the stuffed panda from my computer desk and inspected it. I held my breath, willing him to put it down; it smelled like Scottie. How that was possible was beyond my comprehension, but I made sure to keep it away from anything that could ruin it.

I grabbed the panda from Danny and put it back on the desk, then grabbed my phone and started to walk out of the room. Danny followed, still grinning.

"You grabbed it with a bit more excitement than I'm used to seeing, that's why I was asking," he said, following behind me down the stairs. "It's also cute seeing you act like a lovestruck schoolgirl again, and even better you're acting like it over a guy who is actually decent."

I scoffed and wandered into the kitchen, searching for something sweet. I was more than annoyed that my period started this morning, but it gave some clarity into how I acted last night, sans sex chocolate. My period turned me into a human who insisted on two things; orgasms and candy.

Scottie had gotten a taste of it last night, and I was determined to hide away in my room for the week until I wasn't a hazard to my own sexual needs.

I grabbed a pack of Thin Mints I stashed in the freezer and turned to face Danny. "You don't know what I look like when I'm lovestruck."

"Oh? Eighth grade, Noah McHaven passed you a note asking to be his girlfriend. It lasted for a week, and you brought him homemade cookies everyday," Danny said.

I opened the sleeve of cookies. "That's probably why he broke up with me, I can't bake for shit."

"Then there was Cameron Ansel in ninth grade who asked you to homecoming. You dated him for four months and left love notes in his locker."

"A bit clingy if I do say so myself." I leaned against the island and held out the cookies. "Want one?"

Danny shook his head, and I shrugged, narrowing my eyes. "What about Maverick? I never looked like that with him?"

It was an innocent question. I liked to think that at some point, early on I did love him. In a way that any fifteen-year-old loves anyone, it wasn't ever serious in the grand scheme of things. But hadn't I been happy?

His face fell, his brows pulled together and my heart hurt at the darkness in his eyes. I'd only seen Danny like this one other time, and the look wasn't directed toward me. "I know we've talked about it before, what happened with you guys but I can't help but still feel angry at him Bri." He took a breath. "I never said anything about Maverick to you in high school because you genuinely thought he was a good guy and anything I said would have only caused a rift between us. But thinking about all the times he'd put you down, or make a comment about something you liked and you'd just shut down? No. I don't think you ever looked like you loved him."

"In all honesty, it hurt seeing you try and shove yourself into whatever box he wanted you to fit in."

My hand tightened around the sleeve of cookies, crumbling some of them. I set them down on the counter and went to grab a bottle of water from the fridge.

"And now? You think I look lovestruck?" I asked, something *tugging* in my stomach, like I was both parts terrified and excited about his next words

Danny moved closer and stole a cookie. "You're the most in love I've ever seen you be, and this time I can't help but think it's real and not some random, fleeting feeling."

I shook my head, determined to think about this conversation later when my heart doing somersaults. "You're crazy." I cleared my throat. "Can we change the subject please? When are you and Ronny going on your weekend getaway? I miss Mr. Moo."

Danny grinned. "Next month I've got something planned. It'll be a Friday morning to Sunday night situation. Will that be okay? I can bring him over here."

"Yeah, just give me the exact dates and I'll be here."

His phone dinged in his pocket, he pulled it out as I shoved another cookie into my mouth. A cramp hit me as I swallowed, and I tried my best to look like I hadn't just been assaulted by my own body. Danny typed away at his phone before shoving it into his pocket and grabbing another cookie.

"I gotta get going. Ronny has something cool at home

he wants to show me, I'll see you when I see you," he said as he walked down the hallway.

When the front door shut, I sagged against the counter, my forehead laying on the cool granite. My phone buzzed again in my pocket, and I finally reached for it, keeping my cheek against the counter as the inside of my legs cramped.

It was a bunch of texts from Scottie, and a missed call.

SCOTTIE

We landed! Fucking finally! I'm ready to be home and snuggle with you on the couch, wanna watch The Proposal again?

I thought you were picking me up? Wasn't that the plan? If I'm wrong well….wanna come get me anyway?

Case said I couldn't wait at here…too many stares and honestly it's fine. There's no good places for food. Catching a ride with him be there soon!

The missed call came in between the last two texts, but he didn't leave a message to listen to. It would have probably been him rambling about how the flight was or him telling me about a hot woman he sat next too. I bit the inside of my cheek and pushed the latter idea from my mind before texting him back.

Damn, and here I was getting ready to head to the airport now. Thought you were getting in later.

I'll have this man turn the car around,
don't play with me.

How far from the airport are you?

We're almost at the house. So, not too
late to turn around.

You wouldn't make that poor man drive all
the way back just to have me pick you up.

My phone rang with an unknown number a moment later, and I answered with furrowed brows. I hated spam calls almost as much as I hated peanut butter and jelly sandwiches.

"Hello?"

"Hey Briar, it's Case. Can you *please* tell Scottie you were joking. He's about ready to dial the cops and tell them I kidnapped him."

"Scottie don't touch the door!" a female voice called.

"And they'll believe me! I'm a high profile—" Scottie yelled in the background.

The desperation in Case's voice was comical, and I *almost* laughed. "Please? We're about to turn the corner."

There was a muffled sound before Scottie spoke. "Hey Clover girl, you miss me?"

I chuckled. "Clearly not as much as you missed me. Let Case bring you home, okay?"

"But the airport—"

That same female voice from a moment ago spoke up. "Listen to her, Scottie! Do you really want Case to do all this driving in his condition?"

"I'm fine, sunshine," Case said in a low voice.

Another cramp hit me and I shut my eyes. I, I wasn't technically supposed to start for another two days according to my calendar. But when did women's bodies conform to dates society made up?

"I'll pick you up next time, Hot Shot. Bring flowers and everything."

He mumbled something before the line went dead. I grabbed the cookies and hobbled upstairs to find some more medicine. The bottle I grabbed this morning only had one pill in it and I assumed there'd be more somewhere in the house, there had to be, given that Scottie was busted and bruised after most games. The door opened downstairs as I rifled through the linen closet and didn't bother to go down to greet him.

Another twinge of pain ripped through me and I dropped my hand to rub my lower stomach. I felt Scottie behind me before I saw him and his arms wrapped around my waist before he hugged me from behind. His nose nudged itself into my hair and he took a long, slow inhale.

"It's good to be home," he said before stepping away. I turned around and watched as his brows furrowed as he took in the mess of towels behind me. "Looking for something?"

"Some more medicine. I thought there would be some more laying around but it looks like I'll have to run out and get some. Do you want anything while I'm out?"

"What do you need medicine for, you okay? Why don't I come with you?"

I stepped away, suddenly aware of how close we were standing. My body grew hot and uncomfortable for a different reason, and I bit the inside of my cheek.

"No that's okay," I said, lowering my head.

Scottie huffed and crossed his arms, but I didn't raise my head. Because then I'd see how his shirt bunched around his arms, and I was not in a good place to handle that. I'd want to climb him like a tree and do things that I would regret in the morning—and I wasn't even concerned about that train of thought. Stupid hormones.

He placed his forefinger and thumb under my chin to lift my face until his eyes bore into mine. "Do you really not want to hang out with me?"

I bit my lower lip only to have him glide his thumb over it to release it.

"Just say the word and I'll stay here," he said.

Pressure built in my lower stomach, and I couldn't tell if it was because I was turned on or if it was another cramp trying to destroy me. Either way, I let out a whimper and watched as his eyes darkened.

I pulled away, my skin cold from where he was touching me, and sighed. "You're driving."

He nodded and turned on his heel. I followed behind him, making sure to keep my distance because I wasn't in my right mind to be a responsible, abstinent adult.

Within fifteen minutes we were at the corner store and Scottie followed right behind me. I made a left toward the hygiene products. Might as well stock up while I was here. I wasn't expecting Scottie to continue to follow me though, the back of his hand brushing against mine as he came to walk beside me.

"You don't have to come with me," I said with hot cheeks.

"I haven't seen you for two weeks, god forbid I missed you and want to walk beside you," he said, turning toward me to wink.

I rolled my eyes and turned the corner. Scottie wasn't fazed by the shelves of various brands of tampons, pads, and similar products. He stood beside me as I scanned the shelves, looking for the only brand I trusted. It wasn't until I looked up and saw the last box, shoved at the back of the top shelf. I blew a strand of hair from my face and slowly turned toward Scottie who was staring at me. Smiling, and not in a weird way, but it did make me wonder what was on his mind.

"Need some help?" he asked.

I nodded and pointed to the shelf. "Can you grab those for me? The purple box, I can't reach it."

Scottie reached over me, and I was overwhelmed by the familiar smell of peppermint. I almost leaned back into his chest, but he moved before I had the chance to make that mistake. With the box in his hands, he started walking away, and I tried to grab them from him.

"Give it."

"No," he said, making his way toward the medicine.

"Well they're mine, so let me carry them."

Scottie grabbed the largest bottle of pain medicine they had and continued toward the candy aisle. "What kind of candy do you like? Sour? Chocolate?"

He grabbed one of each kind until his hands were full, then we headed to the counter. I scowled at Scottie while he paid, but he either wasn't intimidated or he simply wasn't paying attention because he took the bag from the cashier with a smile and slipped his hand into mine.

My skin heated and my lower stomach twinged, and I knew it had nothing to do with cramps. This wasn't fair, him being a gentleman and buying me tampons, candy, and pain medicine. Danny's earlier words wandered into my mind, and I realized that Maverick never did anything like this for me back then.

When we got back home, I took a much-needed shower, only to cool myself off and get myself together. Scottie insisted we watch a movie and who was I to deny him such a simple thing. It was a coincidence that his coming home aligned with my everything shower routine, I shaved, exfoliated, and used my new pina colada body wash.

I was soft, smelled delicious, and was pain free by the time I got downstairs. Scottie was sitting on the couch, the candy he bought laid out on the coffee table along with two mugs and a heating pad in his lap.

"What's that for?" I asked.

"Your cramps, come on, sit down," he said, patting the spot next to him.

I sat down and made sure to keep a few inches between us, which was pointless because Scottie pulled me into his side until my head was in his lap and my legs were laying flat on the couch. He then placed the heating pad on my stomach and weaved his fingers in my hair as the movie started. I was stunned by his brazen action and tried to sit up, but his fingers started massaging my scalp and I melted into him.

"You really suck at hiding when you're in pain, you know that?"

I reached feebly for some of the chocolates, Scottie placed them in my hand, and I focused on unwrapping it. "And you could have just let me do my own thing. You know you don't have to baby me right?"

"You call this babying you?" he asked with a raised brow. "Because I call it being a good boyfriend."

I scoffed and turned toward the movie, my body

heating under his touch until I was forced to pull away from him, or tried to anyway. Scottie held me there, not rough or with force. If anything, I misjudged my ability to be a strong woman who didn't need a man. His fingers continued, and I knew the heat in my stomach wasn't from the pad laying across it. I shuffled my legs together, seeking out some kind of friction.

I needed to leave, my breath hitched when Scottie gripped my hair at the base of my neck and gave it a tug.

"Your skin is looking flushed. Need something?" he asked, his own breath heady.

I shook my head and went to move, only to have my hand brush against where he was straining against his pants. A cramp had me letting out a gasp and Scottie ran his hand along my stomach.

"Tell me to stop and I will," he said, blue eyes. "I meant what I said last night about wanting to help. How bad are your cramps?"

"The medicine helped but"—I looked away—"they're still uncomfortable."

Everything was uncomfortable, the cramps, the need to be with him, the stupid feelings I could tell were blooming in my heart.

He brushed away a strand of hair and leaned closer, his hand removing the heating pad before returning to my lower stomach. "I can help, if you want me too."

"Why?" I asked.

"This is what fake boyfriends are for right?"

There was something that flashed across his face, but I was in too much pain and too horny to press for answers. Instead, I nodded, reached for the back of his head, and pulled his mouth to mine.

scottie

Briar kissed me in a way I didn't recognize, it was so different from our first night together. The night with cold fingers and snowflakes in her hair, the night we kissed as strangers who needed some fun.

This time she was needy, gasping as she bit my bottom lip, begging for entrance. My tongue fought with hers as I shifted myself until I was hovering over her. I tossed the heating pad away and ran my hand along the side of her body, reveling in her soft skin before I cradled her neck. I knew I shouldn't be doing this, touching her, kissing her —we hadn't had any real discussions about where we should take our fake relationship, and I wanted to start off on a good note if we made it real. But I'd been thinking about doing this more than what would be considered a healthy amount. So I—a man—wasn't going to push her away when she was as desperate for me as I was her.

What did Briar do after not responding last night? Did she go to sleep? Or did she touch herself, and if so, what did she think about?

I hoped it was me, because I'd been thinking about her saying my name—my real name, not Hot Shot. I slid my hand under the hem of her yellow sleep shorts, but she paused, grabbing my hand and pulling away. Her brows furrowed a fraction, just enough to hint at a crease between them, that's where I placed a kiss.

"Let me get a towel," I said.

Briar's cheeks went red, her eyes darted toward the couch, and I waited. It was obvious she was thinking about something, so I peppered light kisses over her neck and exposed collarbone while she worked out her thoughts. I wasn't in any rush, making her feel good went above my own needs.

"If you don't want to, we don't have to do anything," she said, her voice quiet.

I was lying on top of her, her legs framed my waist, and I adjusted my arms so my weight wasn't completely on her. "What's wrong?" I asked.

Her hips bucked up, but I remained still. "It's just—it's dirty. I'm not thinking straight and it's not fair for me to ask—"

My lips met hers, a command to be quiet. "If you don't want to do anything we don't have too." I kissed the space behind her ear. "You're not dirty Clover, and nothing you ask of me would be unfair."

"Yes it would. This isn't real, not as real as I want it to be," she said, her voice dropping into a whisper.

That got me to stop. The grip this woman had on me was real, whether she knew it or not was beyond me. I'd be as real or fake as she wanted without question if it meant I got to be with her at the end of the day.

"How real do you want it to be? Whatever you want I'll give it to you Clover. All you have to do is say the word."

She bit her bottom lip and shifted to sit up, I sat back on my heels, keeping my hands on her legs.

"I'm going to go to bed," she said, her voice barely above a whisper. "I'm sorry."

When she met my gaze my heart broke, her eyes were glassy and her bottom lip quivered. I grabbed her hand and kissed the back of it before smiling. "I'll see you in the morning."

Briar grabbed the heating pad from where it laid on the floor, grabbed a handful of candy and darted up the stairs.

———

"I can't believe you kissed her," Townes said with crossed arms. Hollis and Hayley were walking ahead of us, bags in hand from the stores they'd already been to. I decided to tag along for their morning errands before Hayley got dropped off with me so the two love birds could go on a much-needed date.

I took a bite of my waffle cone and let out a heavy sigh. "Hey, she kissed me first."

I hoped it wouldn't be the last time either. Maybe next time the opportunity presented itself *I* would kiss Briar first. God look at me, I went from living the bachelor lifestyle to pining over a pretty redhead who had the most stunning smile I'd ever seen.

I wouldn't have it any other way.

"What's next huh? Are you going to confess how you feel?" Townes and I stopped walking while the girls went into another store.

"Should I? I don't want to go too fast and scare her off. Tell me what to do, you're the smarter one," I said.

Townes scoffed and ran a tattooed hand through his hair. "Me? The smart one? You know damn well how things went down between me and Hollis, maybe you should ask Case."

"Ask the guy who was willing to friend zone himself until eternity because he didn't want to have a conversation with Basil?"

Townes and I stared at each other before I hung my head and chuckled. "Okay so none of us know what we're doing half the time, but at least you both got your happily ever after. That's what I want, how do I get it?"

The girls came out of the store, and I swore Townes's eyes lit up when he saw them. It never got old—seeing that stoic man melt for the girls in his life. He looped his arm around Hollis's waist when they reached us and pulled her in for a kiss.

"Ew!" Hayley squealed, covering her eyes.

I couldn't help but laugh. Townes told me a while ago that she was becoming more sensitive to anything *lovey dovey* so he made it a point to do it more often—especially since she didn't listen to his pleas to stop being dramatic about it.

"Uncle Scottie, can we please leave them here? Can I live with you again cause you kiss girls but at least you don't do it in front of my face," Hayley said, tugging on my shirt.

Townes and Hollis broke away laughing.

"You know he only does this because you act like it's a big deal right?" Hollis asked as Townes took her bags. "Maybe if you stopped, then he'd stop too."

Hayley shook her head. "Well maybe Uncle T is just a butt!"

Townes raised a brow. "Do you really want to continue this conversation?"

Hollis and I looked at each other, curious how this was going to play out. Hayley was getting older and with it her attitude was changing in ways we hadn't expected. It was somewhat amusing seeing Townes go full dad mode because while he was always serious with everyone, he rarely pulled out the same attitude with Hayley.

She shook her head, then hung it. "No. I'm sorry."

Townes got down to her level and started speaking in a low voice, I turned to Hollis and threw my arm over her shoulder.

"Can I pick your brain about something?"

She smiled. "Of course."

"Okay so what does it mean when a girl kisses you first, then gets shy and runs off? And you think she might have feelings for you, but you haven't talked to her about it yet."

Hollis blinked, staring at me for a moment before she shook her head slightly and sighed. "I think it means you need to talk to this girl, especially since you have feelings for her."

"So. Don't kiss her again until we talk?"

"Absolutely don't do that Scottie," Hollis said with a serious expression I'd never seen on her face before. "And bring her flowers. Briar likes white roses."

I nodded along as she spoke, then grinned when she finished. "I should have asked you first instead of your husband, you've got all the answers."

Hollis laughed as the other two walked up to us. Townes grabbed her hand and pulled her out of my grip, then gave Hayley a stern look. "Behave for Uncle Scottie, and you"—he looked at me with furrowed brows—"don't place anymore bets with her. I'm out almost two-hundred bucks because she's now gambling in school."

I threw Hayley a wink. "No problem dude, no bets. Promise, now you two go off and have fun. I'll make sure she gets dinner and all the good stuff."

We all said our goodbyes before I directed Hayley back to the parking garage. "So Haybug, you hungry?"

———

Briar hadn't responded to my text I sent when I took Hayley to get food, I flipped my phone over and scanned the message, maybe she did get back to me and I accidentally deleted the message before reading it?

ME

Need me to grab you anything on the way home?

It was a simple question, one I'd ask anyone who was on their period. My sisters would always ask me to grab them candy or drinks, it was why I grabbed Briar so much last night. I wasn't aware of her comfort foods yet, but I was glad she took something before turning in for the night.

Three dots appeared for a moment before disappearing in the text thread, I groaned and put my phone face down on the table and Hayley raised a brow. Beads clicked together at the ends of her braids as she reached for her soda.

"What's wrong, Uncle Scottie?"

"Nothing Haybug, just girl problems."

She smirked and leaned back in the booth. "You know, I can help with that," she said.

I scoffed. "I don't think so."

"I helped Uncle T and Hollis, I can help you," she said with a shrug.

I leaned forward and finished off my burger, contemplating if I was really going to ask a child for relationship advice after I talked to Hollis.

Eh. Why not.

"And how exactly did you help them huh? Oh please give me your words of wisdom," I said, throwing my hands outward. Townes and Hollis had gotten together of their own volition. The only thing Hayley had done was place a bet on when they'd fall in love.

Was I still upset about forking up a decent amount of cash to a child?

Yes, but that was beside the point.

Hayley ran a hand through her braids and raised a brow. "I'll tell you my secrets if, and only if, you sneak me some brownies."

"Townes cut you off again?" I snorted.

"He said too much of a good thing isn't good for me, but Uncle Scottie, they're *so good*. I need them."

I chuckled and nodded. Ever since Case had gotten the brownie recipe from Basil's favorite cafe, everyone has been begging him to make them. A task he did with a smile whenever he had the time.

"Okay so here's my problem; I like this girl and I think

she likes me back, but she hasn't told me. Hollis said I should tell her my feelings and bring her flowers."

Hayley shook her head and waved her hands. "Hold up." She placed her hands under her chin and raised a brow. "What are we dealing with exactly? Do you like her cause she's pretty or cause of her personality and her looks are average? Because you shouldn't settle for ugly people, Uncle Scottie."

I couldn't help but smile. "Trust me Hayley, she's the farthest thing from ugly," I said, my voice low as I thought of clear blue eyes and red hair. Freckles that formed their own constellations on pale skin, and a cute nose decorated with that small piece of jewelry I found myself being drawn too. She changed it almost every other week and I liked seeing how she decorated her cute nose.

"Anyway, my problem has nothing to do with her looks, it's that I'm worried she just doesn't like me back and that I'm overthinking everything. Like, I swear she's giving me signs, but what if this is how I find out I'm illiterate and can't read as well as I thought I could?"

Hayley blinked those big brown eyes and started laughing.

"What? This isn't funny! Keep it up and I'll make sure you never get any brownies ever again."

That sobered her up. Hayley shut her mouth and cleared her throat. "Sorry. It's funny."

"Care to explain?" I asked, dipping a fry a little too aggressively into my ketchup.

She nodded. "First, I'm not sure what illiterate means. Second, if she didn't like you then why is she still talking to you? Raphael at school said boys bother girls they like so maybe it's the other way around?"

I dropped my fry as my brows pulled together. "Okay,

we're tabling my problem for a minute." I crossed my arms. "Haybug, you do know that what he said isn't true right? Boys should never be mean or bother you if they like you. If you tell them to fuck off, then they need to listen. Have you told Hollis or Townes?"

She nodded. "Hollis said I should give them a wet willy if they don't leave me alone and Uncle T promised to show up at school and make the boys pee their pants. But I think it's different for girls cause Hollis used to talk to Uncle T *all* the time when he was scowly and now they're married."

I contemplated her reasoning for half a second before shaking my head. Why was I taking dating advice from a nine-year-old again?

"That's different," I said with a wave of my hand.

She shrugged. "I don't think so, but I think you should keep being yourself. If she doesn't like you, it's her loss and you should find a girl who is more pretty."

Be myself. Buy her flowers. I had a lot of options to consider.

We finished our lunch and headed home, Hayley hummed to herself in the backseat—a habit she picked up from Hollis—and pointed curiously to Briar's car in the driveway.

"Do you know who that is?" she asked.

"Yeah, my roommate," I said, parking my car next to hers.

Hayley hopped out and inspected the red Volkswagen Beetle. "It's not a very pretty color, and it's girly."

I coughed through a laugh and made my way to the door. Hayley pushed past me, running down the hall to the kitchen and throwing her backpack onto the table like she used to when she and Townes lived here. As I walked to meet her, I watched as Hayley spun toward the living room and paused. Her mouth dropped open, she looked at me and pointed at something.

"She's your roommate?" Hayley asked. Loudly.

Briar giggled from the living room and the sound had my feet moving faster. I had to see her, see the way her nose scrunched and her eyes closed. She had been in her room this morning when I left, and ignored my offer to make her pancakes. Call me desperate, but I couldn't go a whole day without seeing her anymore. I needed her attention, would get on my knees for it.

I entered the kitchen and leaned against the island, keeping my eyes on Briar. Her heating pad was sitting on the couch, along with candy wrappers. I smiled to myself knowing that despite how last night ended, she was a sucker for sweets. Hayley's eyes widened and she smiled like she found the answer to a puzzle. She walked closer and tugged on my shirt, a silent demand to lean down so she could whisper in my ear.

"I don't know who you want to fall in love with you, but you should forget about them. Cause she's *super* pretty."

Briar walked up as Hayley pulled away. My eyes met hers and time seemed to slow. She had her hair in a loose braid, there were marks on her arm that indicated she had taken a great nap, and her smile was bright. Crystal clear blue eyes stared at me and warmth spread through my body.

She knelt down to Hayley's level and smiled. "I'm Briar. You must be Hayley, your uncle has told me so much about you."

"Yeah well he hasn't told me about you like *at all!* He

told me about a girl he likes but she's giving him mixed sig—"

I had never shut that girl up faster.

My hand covered her mouth and I yanked her back toward me, a desperate attempt to save myself from looking ridiculous. Which didn't work because Hayley stomped on my big toe, forcing me to release her and clutch onto the granite countertop.

"That wasn't very nice, Uncle Scottie," Hayley said before rounding the island into the kitchen and grabbing her favorite chips from the pantry. I always kept them on hand for her—sour cream and onion, a flavor I wouldn't buy for myself.

Briar was laughing again, her arms around her stomach as she tried to keep herself from keeling over.

"Yeah, laugh it up while you can." I stood and closed the small distance between us. She peered up at me, but I kept my hands to myself. "Cause soon enough that little girl's going to ask you enough uncomfortable questions you'll wish you could crawl into a hole."

Briar sobered up and stood straighter, turning her attention to my niece who was watching us with curious eyes and sour cream and onion covered fingers.

"So uh, how long are you babysitting? Can we talk?" Briar asked, her voice low as she avoided my gaze. I turned against the island, placing myself next to Briar and a thought ran through me—I wanted to run a finger along the exposed skin between her green crop top and athletic pants.

"A few hours. After that I'm all yours," I said.

Briar smiled, her cheeks a cute shade of pink. She turned toward Hayley. "Do you want to do anything since you're here?" Briar asked, reaching across the island to grab a chip.

Hayley shrugged. "I don't know, maybe just watch movies?"

"Sure, we can do that, go sit down and pick one while I make popcorn okay?" I said.

Briar's gaze swung toward me as Hayley ran into the living room, and I smiled to myself. Call me cocky but I felt luck was going to be in my favor tonight.

CHAPTER 21

briar

The front door closed and I hugged the heating pad closer to my stomach. Townes had picked up Hayley after his date with Hollis, and I was surprised when Hayley put up a fight. Scottie had to wrap her burrito style and take her to the front door, where she and Townes had a conversation about why she couldn't spend the night tonight. It took Scottie promising a sleepover sometime over the summer for her to give up and leave.

She was cute.

Scottie walked back into the kitchen and started cleaning up, I stood to help him, the man made us dinner and offered to make dessert as well. The least I could do was fight through the cramps and help him out. But when I touched a plate on the table, he whipped around and pointed back to the couch.

"Sit down," he said, his voice firm. "You can't even stand up straight right now, go relax and I'll be there in a minute."

When I picked the plate up anyway, Scottie dropped the dishes he was holding in the sink and stormed toward me. A yelp escaped me when he picked me up, his arms under my legs and my hands wrapped around his neck. He carried me to the couch, placed the heating pad over my stomach and tucked my hair behind my ear before kissing my forehead.

"You're going to either sit down on the couch and relax or go upstairs and go to bed."

"You can't make me do anything," I said, flexing my hands and grabbing a scruff of hair at the nape of his neck.

His pupils dilated, something akin to lust taking over the blues in his eyes.

"I know for a fact I can make you do one thing," he mumbled.

Rendered speechless, I watched a movie while Scottie cleaned everything, trying to keep my mind on *Bambi* instead of the heat pooling in my stomach. I'd been stupid last night to push him away, the only reason I did it was because of my period. While Scottie made it obvious that he wasn't bothered, I was.

It was hard to feel confident and sexy when you felt like an alien in your own body. And I didn't take the time to explain that because my horny lady bits weren't going to listen to me reason with Scottie. It was bone or be boned and I wanted to be classy damn it.

Scottie sat beside me, and I felt my cheeks heat. I wanted him closer.

I was a big, horny, hormonal mess.

"Sorry to spring babysitting on you at the last second. Townes asked me earlier when we were out and I can never say no to him," Scottie said, resting his arm across the back of the couch.

I shrugged. "I'm fine with it. Kids are fun, and honestly

she's super funny. I take it she gets it from you? I haven't interacted with Townes that much but he doesn't seem to be much of a comedic influence."

"He's funny in his own way and I can only take partial credit for her humor."

Scottie and I fell into silence, but not before he grabbed my feet and started rubbing the arches again. That man and his magic hands.

Maybe the surge of endorphins was what caused me to have the confidence to tell him what was on my mind.

"About last night…" I tried to sit up, but Scottie pinned me in place with that same heated stare from earlier. "I'm sorry."

His nostrils flared. "What are you sorry about exactly?" My breath hitched as his hand traveled up my leg, stopping to cup the back of my knee before he leaned in. "Tell me to stop if you're uncomfortable."

I was anything but uncomfortable and I had to get my breathing under control before I turned into a literal puddle. "For making you think I didn't want you."

He kissed my collarbone. "Do you?"

"Yes." I breathed, arching into him. "But I'm not ready, I mean h-hold on. Stop."

Scottie released me and sat up, his brows furrowed. "What's wrong?"

"I can't think when you're making it difficult to function with all the touching and kissing," I said. My stomach was in knots, my heart was going to fly out of my chest and my cheeks burned. Scottie grinned and leaned back in, being careful not to touch me.

"But I like touching you, and kissing you? That might be one of my favorite activities, Clover."

"One of them? What's another?" I asked.

"Making you smile," he said, his words finite.

I licked my bottom lip and watched as his gaze tracked the movement. "You can't say stuff like that, Hot Shot."

"Have I ever told you that I love it when you call me that?" Scottie asked.

I pulled my feet away from his grasp, folded them underneath me and moved the heating pad to the coffee table. I crawled into Scottie's lap until my legs were on either side of him. His hands rested on my thighs, and I took a deep breath. This was it, I was going to bare my myself to this crazy, funny man and hope he returned a fraction of my feelings.

"Here's the thing"—I played with the red hair at the nap of his neck—"I don't know what you did to me but I'm not mad about it. You make me laugh, make me food, and make me second guess my past choices in men. Because how could I have thought any of them were good for me when you existed this entire time? I've seen what they say about you online, that you seem happier, and I know this arrangement was supposed to be temporary, but I wouldn't mind if it wasn't. Maybe you like me enough to say fuck it and date me for real? My only condition is, despite how much I want to, we don't have sex again until my period is over. It's messy and there are things I want to do that involve your mouth that's not possible right now."

There it was, I bared myself to him and waited with bated breath for him to respond. Did I read too much into our recent interactions? Did Scottie have feelings for me, or had I gotten too caught up in my own? If Scottie told me he wanted to go back to his previous lifestyle I'd respect that, but it would suck.

Scottie's hands tightened around my thighs before he

pulled me close enough to feel how hard he was under me.

"Is that okay?" I asked when I got anxious about how long it was taking him to respond.

He smiled. "Clover girl, it's more than okay. I don't want you to ever doubt yourself when you tell me how you feel, especially not when I feel the same. You make me want to be better, to be good enough to give you all the things you want."

"You don't even know what that is," I said, trying to contain a smile. Scottie and I hadn't had any of the tough topics; marriage, kids, what kind of pets we would have, but I was willing to tackle those topics one by one as they came our way.

He chuckled and shook his head. "I'm sure I'll say yes anyway. I do have one question though." One of his hands traveled to my waistband. "Are you *sure* we have to wait? Because I don't care about earning some red wings, all I care about is making you feel good."

I threw my head back in laughter and my phone dinged at the same time. I got off of Scottie's lap and made sure to push my butt out a tiny bit when I bent over to unplug my phone from the charger.

DANNY

Doesn't he look dapper in his dinosaur costume?

The picture was of Mr. Moo in a vibrant purple T-Rex costume. His tongue was sticking out as he was cradled by Ronny, who wore a matching dinosaur shirt.

Too cute for words.

Ugh I know! Anyway I was wondering
when a good day to drop him off was?
We're leaving next weekend, does
Thursday night sound good?

Honestly whenever you want to drop him
off is fine with me. Scottie has a home
game on Thursday night but I will make
sure I'm at home.

You're a life saver. I'll text you when I
know what time I'm leaving, Ron here is
keeping almost everything a secret
from me.

Scottie was staring at my ass when I turned around and I swayed my hips when I walked back toward him. He stopped me when I stood in front of him, dragging his hands up the back of my thighs.

"Who was that?" he asked, kissing my stomach.

"Danny. He's dropping his dog off next week while him and his boyfriend go out of town."

Scottie made a noncommittal noise before kissing me again. "So how long is my pretty girlfriend making me wait before I'm allowed to ravage her?"

I placed my hands on his shoulders and suppressed a shiver when his mouth grazed over a sensitive spot. "Girlfriend?"

"Yes. Girlfriend, and not pretending like we've been doing for stupid pictures and press." Scottie pulled me closer and gazed up at me, my eyes were locked with him and my heart soared. "Now can I please know when I can shove my head between your thighs again? I'm going crazy just thinking about it."

I chuckled and leaned down to kiss him, warmth spreading in my chest knowing we weren't pretending anymore.

briar

I'd been in the middle of getting ready for Scottie's game when my phone rang from where I'd placed it on the bathroom counter. I set down the orange eyeliner pencil and tapped the speaker icon.

"Hey! We are on our way with Mr. Moo! Do you have everything set up?" Danny asked over the loud engine in the background.

I made a trip to the pet store earlier and got everything I needed from puppy pads, extra blankets, and soft dog chews. Danny was going to bring over Mr. Moo's various medications and his dog bed, but otherwise the house was dog proof and the old chihuahua was going to have a great weekend with us.

"Everything is good to go! The door will be open so feel free to just come inside, okay?"

Scottie had left a few hours ago, and I was going to take Mr. Moo with me once I was done. There was no way I'd leave that senior dog alone in a new environment. I had a great track record with him, and I refused to end up on that old man's shit list. I finished writing Scottie's jersey number on my face at the same time the doorbell rang.

I hurried to the door. "I thought I told you the door would be—oh—hey Ronny," I said.

The only different between Ronny and Danny was Ronny had way more tattoos, spanning both arms and the back of his neck. Otherwise, they shared the same bald, bearded look. Ronny held Mr. Moo under his arm as he flashed a grin and waved. "Hey Bri! Sorry, the little guy here had an accident on Danny and he's busy cleaning up himself *and* the car."

I waved him inside. "No worries!"

Mr. Moo had no teeth and was missing an eye, the other bulged out of his head slightly, giving him a pathetic, yet cute look. I reached for him and scrunched my nose when he licked my cheek. "Hi buddy. Ready to spend time with your favorite aunt?"

Ronny set down the bag that was slung over his shoulder before following me into the living room. "You're his only aunt."

"What about Veronica?" I asked, referencing Danny's older sister.

"Oh, Moo here hates her. He pissed on her Gucci bag once when she didn't give him peanut butter and then tore off his diaper in the middle of the night. She called us screaming cause he shit *everywhere*, including her bed. How he got up there we never figured out."

I couldn't help but laugh.

"Okay so Danny texted you about his medication, right? How much he takes and when?"

"Yes, he also gave me a list of side effects and what to do if Moo here is having issues. I also have your vet's number saved in my phone."

Ronny had been holding tension in his shoulders, and I'd only realized it when his whole body relaxed. He recovered quickly though and drew a tattooed hand through his beard.

"Alright well you've got everything handled then. I better get going, help Danny clean up the seat before we head out."

"I'm so happy you guys are getting away, and I know Danny is more than excited."

There was a twinkle in Ronny's eyes, full of emotions I couldn't place because he was waving and walking back outside before I could ask any more questions. I turned to Moo and placed my hands on my hips when he lifted a leg over a pair of Scottie's running shoes.

"Guess he won't miss those too much huh?"

I spent time with Moo outside, letting him explore the yard and kept him away from the patio furniture. Only because I was afraid he'd pee on that too and I didn't feel like cleaning more than I had too. Scottie's shoes were already in the washer, along with an old blanket Mr. Moo confused for his bed. His bladder was significantly weaker than I remembered, and I put a diaper on him after he peed in the kitchen.

Moo looked at me with that ridiculous face of his, tongue out and shaking as he walked up to me. Limping because he wanted sympathy and a treat.

"You're such a pick me," I said under my breath as I handed over a treat.

Once Mr. Moo was satisfied, I put his things in my bag, then put on a fabric baby carrier that Ronny left and headed out to the car. When we got to the arena, I placed Mr. Moo in the carrier and made my way inside. Dogs weren't allowed inside unless they were service dogs, but the Chihuahua was small enough that he passed for a baby bundled in a blanket. I wandered to the athletics area where I found dad talking with a woman I'd never seen before. She wore a navy suit, her black hair was pulled into a low bun, and her thick frame glasses suited her slim face well.

Dad turned toward me and raised an arm. "There she is! We were just talking about you," he said.

"Oh?" I stood next to him and smiled at the woman. "Whatever he said about me, especially if it's embarrassing, probably isn't true."

She laughed. "Goodness no. He was telling me about your brilliance behind the piece you've been doing of the team. He sent me your information and I plan on checking out your work. I'm Camry by the way, I work in operations for the network. It was nice meeting you," she said before turning toward dad. "We'll be in touch soon."

Dad rubbed my shoulder and pulled away with a smile, he was on the verge of saying something until he noticed the dog. "Is that what I think it is?"

"Don't talk about him like he can't understand what you're saying," I said, patting Mr. Moo's head.

"That makes him more terrifying. Anyway, I'm glad I caught you before the game! I wanted to go over things with you." I followed him as he walked toward the locker room. The game was starting soon, and I knew all the players would be in full gear by now. "I'm not sure what you and Scottie were doing, but the media is obsessed about you two. Moreso than we thought they would be."

"Oh? That's good," I said, keeping my eyes forward. If Dad noticed the blush I felt creeping up my cheeks he'd get suspicious, and I wasn't interested in what kind of conversation would follow.

We reached the door to the locker rooms and Dad faced me with a smile. "Keep up the good work kiddo, and at this point you and Lancaster can end things anytime. Let me know so I can get with the social media manager. It'll blow over quickly, but I don't want you to experience any potential fallout. Sound good?"

My mouth went so dry. I couldn't confess the truth to him. I didn't want him to figure out like this that Scottie and I made things official a few days ago. I'd tell him over dinner or something, with Scottie, and he could give us both the talk about how he's too young for grandchildren.

"Sounds good Dad, good luck tonight," I said with a smile.

After he disappeared behind the door, I made my way to the family room where I knew Basil was waiting for me. I flashed my badge at a security guard and was let inside. I immediately spotted Basil by the snack table.

Her attention darted to Mr. Moo. "Oh my gosh. He's so cute!"

Mr. Moo wiggled against my chest at her enthusiasm as his tongue flopped around while she pet him. "Be honored Basil, he doesn't usually like strangers."

"He makes me miss my old dog," she said, her expression falling a fraction before lighting up again. "But I made Case promise me we could get a pet after this season's over. I'm considering taking a break from coaching, so I need someone at home to keep my company."

We walked over to a couple seats and settled in as the game started. Women and children stood all around us, in their own worlds while watching their partners.

"So how are things between you and Scottie?" Basil asked, not meeting my gaze.

There was something in her tone that threw me off. I

sat forward and tried to make her look at me. When she didn't, I lightly pinched her leg. "What do you know?" I asked.

Basil pinched me back. "Not much."

"But enough to act suspicious. Spill Whitlock," I said.

Basil smiled. "Fine, *fine.* The other night Scottie kept blowing up Case's phone while we were *busy* and I had enough. I was going to call and yell at him until I saw what was so urgent."

"Well?" I asked, petting Mr. Moo to ease my anxiety.

"He was just telling Case that you two made things official, there was some other stuff in there that's not important but Briar"—Basil grabbed my hands—"I'm really happy for you."

I bit my bottom cheek and cast a quick glance to the ice below us right as Scottie flung the puck into the opposing team's net. The crowd cheered as music played, and my heart soared in my chest. I was proud of him; for being a great player, for being true to himself and loving his friends and family, and I was proud of us both for choosing each other.

I was four throws in, down so many points I'd lost count, and confident enough to think I could make a comeback. Scottie stood behind me, his hands firmly on my hips and ready to help me aim the dart at the board. Really, he wanted an excuse to touch me and who was I to deny him? Mr. Moo slept against my chest; his soft snores drowned out by the music surrounding us.

I threw the dart and cheered with Basil and Hollis when it landed dead center.

"I knew you could do it!" Hollis squealed.

"I doubted you, but you proved me wrong and I'm so proud," Basil said as she gave me a hug. We were all a little more than tipsy, and our guys had stayed by our sides the entire night.

Our guys. It was so weird to think that, but I couldn't be happier.

"Shit are you crying? I'm sorry. I was just joking, I never doubted you," Basil said in a panic, her hands rubbing my arms as I blinked away tears.

A laugh bubbled out of me and I reached for her hands, bringing them to her sides. "It's not that, it's just"— I reached for Hollis's hand and pulled her into my drunken girl huddle—"you're both so nice and I'm so happy I met you!"

We were a fit of happy tears and giggles, and our little bubble was broken by Maverick. He walked up with who I assumed was his girlfriend, she was an inch taller than him and had short red hair.

What were the chances three redheads would be in the same place?

Scottie laid an arm over my shoulders and nodded toward his equipment manager. "Sup," he said.

Maverick smiled at me and it felt wrong. "I figured I'd introduce you too to Emily since our double date got cancelled."

Scottie tensed beside me. "We rescheduled for tomorrow; you couldn't wait to introduce us until then?"

I elbowed his side and took a step forward, keeping one hand on the sleeping dog on my chest. "Don't mind him, he's just upset I kicked his butt in darts. I'm Briar."

Emily and I shook hands. "It's nice to meet you, now if you'll excuse us, I need to drag Mav here back to the dance floor. He didn't want to pass up on talking to you guys before we left. See you tomorrow!"

We watched as she dragged Maverick back to the crowd on the dance floor, and once they were gone, I spun on Scottie, crossing my arms.

"What was that about?" I asked.

He pulled me toward him by the loops in my pants, but I could only get so close with the dog between us. "I don't know what you're talking about," he said.

"You were a little rude just now." I let out a shaky breath as Scottie dragged his fingers up my back.

"Well sue a guy for not liking his girl's ex, especially when he's looking at her like he still wants her."

I pushed away from him with furrowed brows. "He doesn't want me."

Scottie made noise in the back of his throat and leaned down until his nose brushed against my hair. "I'd like to go home and show you how much I want you. How does that sound Clover?"

A tingle went down my spine and I stood straighter in his arms. I placed a kiss on his cheek and smiled even though he couldn't see me, I whispered in his ear, "Get me out of here Hot Shot."

briar

Scottie couldn't usher me into the house fast enough. His hand was at the small of my back as he shut the door behind us. When he faced me, his smile fell, and he pointed at Mr. Moo.

"What are we going to do about him?" he asked.

I laughed and undid the carrier, startling the small dog awake. "We need to do his bedtime routine, then get him set up in the pen."

"What pen?" Scottie asked, following me into the kitchen.

I set Mr. Moo down and let him wander while I got his medication and dinner ready. The alcohol was wearing off and I felt a headache building. "It's upstairs in the guest bathroom. It was the only place big enough I could find that didn't have carpet. He doesn't wear the diaper at night," I said. "I'll be done getting him settled in a minute if you want to find a movie to watch? Or a game we can play?"

Scottie kissed me before narrowing his eyes at Mr. Moo and walking out of the room. It took all of fifteen minutes to get the chihuahua settled for bed. With the bathroom door closed I rushed to my room to change out into something more comfortable.

My new blue nightgown, it had stars on it instead of flowers like my yellow one. I knew tonight that Scottie was going to jump my bones—I wanted him to—especially after I texted him this morning that Aunt Flo packed her bags for the next few weeks. Granted the nightgown might not be the sexiest thing, but I wore it for the easy access.

By the time I got downstairs my headache was gone, my breath was minty fresh, and I was ready to settle in for a long night. When I rounded the corner into the living room though I was stopped short by Scottie, holding up a card game I'd only seen one other time.

"What's this?" he asked with a cocky smile.

Hollis and Basil had forgotten to take the game home with them and never answered my texts about when I could give it back. I'd put it in the hall closet for safe keeping, not expecting Scottie to grab it.

"Spicy truth or dare. I don't know about you, but I think this sounds more fun than a movie," he said.

I shook my head and walked toward where he stood in the kitchen. "You do know that this game only leads to bad decisions, right?"

He kissed my forehead and smirked. "You've never played with me, Clover. Because only good things happen when you play with me."

Scottie grabbed a couple water bottles from the fridge and a bag of chips from the pantry before moving to the living room. I was right behind him with flutters in my stomach and a smile on my face. We faced each other at the coffee table and Scottie had a smirk as he shuffled the cards.

"Who goes first?" he asked.

I shrugged. "Ladies first."

He chuckled and held his hands up, waiting for me to ask him the first question.

"Truth or dare?" I asked, grabbing a chip

"Truth," he said with no hesitation.

I reached for the pile of truth cards and let out a slow breath before I pulled the top card. The question made my cheeks flush, but I had to press on. "What would you like to try in the bedroom?"

Scottie ran his tongue over his teeth as he grinned, and damn if the sight didn't do something to me. I adjusted how I was sitting to ease the growing friction between my legs.

"What haven't I tried I think is the better question," he said.

"So, you're saying you've tried everything there is?"

Scottie leaned forward, bracing himself on his forearms. "Maybe. But I haven't tried a lot with you, and I can't wait to see all the ways I'll make you beg for me to make you come."

Yeah, there was no way I was lasting long if this was how the game was starting. I cleared my throat and put the card off to the side, and without looking at him said, "Dare."

He leaned back and I knew he was still smirking. "Oh this is good," he said through a throaty laugh. "I dare you to give me a sixty second lap dance. Blindfolded."

Well fuck me.

Scottie moved up to sit on the couch and leaned back with his arms behind his head. He raised a brow in challenge, knowing how nervous I was and was relishing in it. I'd never given anyone a lap dance before, and he could tell. I stood on shaky legs, letting false confidence hide my nerves.

"We don't have a blindfold," I said.

"Sure, we do," Scottie said before lifting his hips. The sound of his buckle filled the quiet room. I couldn't look away as he removed his belt. My mouth dried as he held it out to me, veiny hands looking delicious in the low-lit room.

"That's not a blindfold," I said, not taking it.

"I have one in my room if you'd rather take this game upstairs?"

I shook my head and took the belt. It took a second to fix it over my eyes, it wasn't perfect but if I didn't move too much or open my eyes it would work just fine.

"Can you set a timer?" I asked, feeling my way around the coffee table until I stood before him.

Scottie used the voice feature on his phone to set one and the gesture made me smile. He could have lied and said he set a timer, but instead he provided proof he'd done it. I turned until I faced away from him then backed up. His hands found their place on my hips, and I sucked in a breath as I started to move. It wasn't graceful, or sexy, but I felt confident in how I moved and Scottie's hands were responsible for that feeling. He kept me steady as I rolled my hips, bent down until my ass hovered over his crotch. I didn't sit on him, but I got close enough to feel how hard he was in his pants.

The timer rang and I removed myself from his grip, taking off the belt and tossing it onto the couch. I needed a minute to will the heat in my cheeks away before I faced him. When I felt composed, I tossed him a smile before sitting back down.

"It's your turn," I said.

Scottie leaned forward, a dark heat overtaking the blue in his eyes. "Dare."

I pulled a card and laughed. "I dare you to put an ice cube down your pants."

He shook his head and walked to the fridge, without any hesitation in his movements, he grabbed an ice cube and dropped it in his pants. With gritted teeth he walked back over, his hands in fists at his side.

"Pick one please. Truth or dare, just hurry. This is freezing," he said through gritted teeth.

I laughed. "Dare."

Scottie moved closer and didn't bother reaching for a card before he was leaning in, his body heat radiating off of him.

"Take the ice cube out."

I moved slower than he probably wanted, but after this there was no going back. I stood until we were chest to chest, I dragged my hand down the front of his stomach until I reached the waistband of his pants. Scottie's breathing turned erratic, and I felt my nipples harden against his chest as I pushed my hand down. The ice cube was sitting at the bottom of his boxers, but I didn't take it out. Instead, I wrapped my hand around his throbbing cock and tugged.

That was all it took before Scottie broke, he came after me, forcing his tongue into my mouth as he kissed me. I didn't fight him, had no need too, I wanted him just as badly as he wanted me. My body burned under his touch and ignited with every tug on my hair, my lips, my clothes. I wanted more. **Needed** it.

Scottie removed his hands and a whine escaped me, but the moment was fleeting. He kneeled at the edge of the couch and yanked my body toward him before he shifted my nightgown over my hips. A flicker of surprise flashed across his face when he realized I wasn't wearing any underwear. I tried to catch myself on the suede material to keep from falling off the couch, but Scottie's hands held my legs open, making it impossible to move. He kept me steady as his breath caressed over my inner thigh, causing my hips to buck in their awkward position, seeking him out.

A calloused finger ran along my slit and Scottie sucked in a sharp breath.

"Look how wet you are baby." He placed a kiss on my thigh, so far away from where I desperately needed him. "How long have you been like this?"

I moaned when his breath whispered over my clit. "All day," I said.

My mind had been filled with dirty thoughts all day in anticipation for this very moment.

What if he had you *for dinner that night you danced in the living room?*

I wonder if he ever heard me touching myself through the walls.

Why didn't he take the bait when I said there were men better at sex? He could have taken me upstairs—forgotten the aquarium and—

A breathy moan filled the room when Scottie closed the distance, his tongue collecting the pooling wetness before dragging up and flicking over my clit. His hands moved to my hips, locking them down so no matter how much I tried, I couldn't get away.

Scottie *devoured* me. I was so busy trying not to come

with every movement on his tongue I didn't even think to remind him to breathe. Heat pooled low in my stomach, until it traveled down to my legs, pulling heat to that point between my legs that Scottie was attacking.

"I—I'm go—"

He pulled away, and the cool sensation of his disappearance sent shivers wracking through me. I smacked the couch; my frustration made my voice hoarse as I looked at him. "Why'd you do that."

Scottie looked at me with heavy lids, his curls stuck up in different directions—courtesy of my hands. His voice was low, filled with velvety heat that sent a zip through me.

"Did you really think I was going to cut my time short here?" he asked, placing a finger at my entrance, holding my gaze. "I love the little sounds you make Clover, and I'm planning on hearing them all night long."

I gasped when he pushed in and found my clit with his thumb. His other hand gripped my waist while he moved up to kiss me. I moaned into his mouth, tasting myself on his tongue as we kissed. He pulled away and removed his hand at the same time, then held my stare as he sucked his pointer and middle fingers. The sight sent me overboard and I whined when he pushed those two fingers in.

Heat built up again throughout my body as he hit that sensitive spot inside me over, and over again. I needed to come. I'd die if I didn't.

I gripped his wrist, keeping his hand there as I worked my hips.

"Fuck baby, you need it that bad?" he asked, biting my hip. "Take it. Ride my fingers and take what you need."

I was panting, moving faster and faster until tingles started down my legs. It was so close, I was going to—

Scottie removed his hand and the heat disappeared. I covered my eyes with the palms of my hands as a frustrated sob threatened its way out. He gently moved my hands to my side and kissed the tip of my nose. My lids fluttered open and found him staring at me with a fondness that was jarring considering what we were doing.

He brushed my hair behind my ear. "I said I wanted to hear you all night long baby girl. You can't come yet."

My chest heaved as determination made its way through me. I sat up, and shoved Scottie away. He laid on the couch, eyes wide with questions I wasn't going to give him the chance to ask. I moved over him until my legs bracketed his head, and smirked.

"You also told me to take what I needed," I said.

Scottie's eyes darkened before he gripped my hips and pulled me onto his face. I braced my hands on what I could, which wasn't much considering we were on the middle of the couch and Scottie's legs were hanging off.

My hands found his hair, and I rode his face until that familiar heat sparked again. His grip tightened on my hips until I was sure they were going to leave a bruise. It didn't take long for me to fall over the edge. My body stiffened and I let out a groan as my release hit me. Scottie's hold turned soft as I came down and he pressed a kiss to that same spot on my thigh when I released him.

I couldn't help but giggle at seeing his dazed expression. "Sorry. I should have made sure you could breathe before I sat down."

"Don't apologize. It would be an honor to die doing what I love."

I raised a brow and ignored the tingles that shot through my body as his thumb dragged over my thigh. "And what would that be?"

"Eating pussy of course." He winked.

The next thing I knew, I was being lifted off of him and being pushed down into the couch. My ass in the air and Scottie hovering over my back.

"And now I'm going to do my next favorite thing," he said with a kiss to my neck. "Fucking you until there's no doubt in your mind that this pussy"—a wet smack followed the stinging between my legs, and I let out a yelp. That fucker *slapped* my clit—"belongs to me."

scottie

God I wanted to fuck her.

Having Briar on her hands and knees in front of me with her ass in the air was going to send me into cardiac arrest. She looked perfect like this, she is perfect. I knew it, my cock knew it, and hell I wanted to parade her around so *everyone* knew it.

For now, though I'd settle for being selfish and having her all to myself. I slapped her pussy again and kissed her neck as she let out another moan.

"Is this too much?" I asked.

She shook her head, turning her face into the couch and I pulled away. A breathy whine escaped her pretty lips, and I stared at her wet pussy as I stroked myself.

"I need you to use your words," I said, suppressing a shudder.

"It's not too much," she said, her voice muffled by the cushion. "I need you."

Those words broke something in me. The part of me that used to think I wasn't worthy of long-term love, that quick fucks were all I was capable of. But hearing those words from her made me feel I was needed, and she needed me. Almost as much as I needed her.

I leaned down and kissed between her shoulder blades as I rubbed my cock over her clit, it wasn't until she arched against me that I slid inside her. I almost came right then; she was so tight and so wet it was hard to keep my composure.

So I stilled for a moment, peppering kisses over her back while I grabbed her hip. I didn't start moving until she relaxed beneath me, and despite my best efforts to make this last, I couldn't. I pulled out slowly before slamming back into her, eliciting a beautiful sound from her. We were skin against skin, our moans filled the space around us.

At one point Briar couldn't hold herself up anymore, and that was when I pulled out of her and moved us to the floor. Her on her back and me on top of her so I could watch the expressions on her pretty face as I made her feel good. She reached up and clawed at my back, and that only made me move faster.

Briar moaned another release, and I knew I wasn't going to last. She was clutching onto me, and I wasn't strong enough to anchor us both. I placed my forearms on either side of her head and kissed her as I finished.

We were a sweaty, blissful mess on our floor but that didn't stop me from kissing her anywhere I could reach; her neck, her face, her shoulder. When I finally looked at her, my heart expanded so much I didn't think it would fit in my chest anymore.

Her eyelids were heavy, her smile lazy. "Hey Hot Shot."

"Hey Clover girl," I said with another kiss to her nose.

There wasn't anything to say as we laid there together for a long while. Eventually we moved upstairs to my bedroom, Briar washed up in the bathroom and I fluffed a pillow on my bed for her to use. I welcomed her in my arms when she settled beside me, and for the first time since our snowy night together I had a restful sleep.

———

"Where are you taking me?" Briar asked.

I walked beside her, my fingers laced with hers as I led her toward our destination. She wore a blindfold—one of my old ties because my belt wasn't appropriate out of the house—and stayed close to my side as we walked down the sidewalk.

"It's a surprise," I said.

"I'm not super into surprises though," she said, clinging to my arm.

I chuckled and continued forward. We were almost there, and I wished for a moment we could stay like this longer. This morning I reminded Briar of our double date with Maverick and despite my reservations about sharing her attention, I promised I'd be on my best behavior. I planned this activity two months ago and at the last second insisted Maverick tag along, I hoped he'd be too busy to pay us any attention.

I opened the door to the studio and took off the makeshift blindfold. Briar blinked and I was more than excited to see her reaction. Four large oak tables were centered in the middle of the room with bowls, vegetables, and hot plates lined on top of them. There were a few people chatting amongst themselves, but I didn't see Maverick, not yet anyway.

Briar faced me and I adjusted her glasses so they sat higher on the bridge of her nose. She'd switched out her septum ring for a silver bumble bee and put on makeup—I hadn't seen her wear any since the wedding.

"What is this place?" she asked.

"Cooking lessons," I said with a grin. I'd felt horrible after the incident with the potatoes, then for leaving her to fend for herself when I was away with the team. I didn't mind making meals for her, but I also knew how much she liked to be independent so I was more than willing to help in any way I could.

She raised a brow and crossed her arms. "Why?"

"Because you can't cook? I'm sorry, is this a bad idea? I don't mind cooking for you, but I thought you'd like to learn. We can leave and do something else," I said.

Briar's mouth twitched at the side, like she was holding back a smile. She inhaled and straightened her shoulders, leveling me with a stare. "Scottie this is perfect. As much as I love your cooking, I realize I need to learn, but don't stop leaving me meals. Okay? Those are one of my favorite parts about my day."

I leaned down and kissed her cheek. "I promise that after this class I won't expect you to cook, and I'll leave you meals. Can't have my girl slaving away over a hot stove if she doesn't have to."

"Hey guys!" a grating voice sounded behind us.

I slipped my hand into Briar's before turning to face Maverick and his girlfriend. There was something off about her hair and it bugged me more than it should have. She wore jeans and an oversized shirt while Maverick wore something more business casual. His jeans were dark and his buttoned shirt and slicked back hair were more appropriate for some kind of meeting rather than a cooking class. He moved to pull Briar in for a hug, and I couldn't help but block him, a smile on my face.

"Nice to see you two made it! I hope neither of you avoid meat because we're learning how to make steak," I said.

Emily smiled. "Oh fun! Come on hon let's grab a table."

With Briar behind me, I grabbed our own table, right next to theirs, and made sure to put myself between them. I never thought I'd be the jealous type, but it was easy to do when Maverick was being a dick at work and looking at Briar like he still wanted her.

"Why are you acting like he's infected with something?" Briar asked.

I looped my pinky around hers and grinned. "He might be, I'm just being cautious."

Briar rolled her eyes as she smirked and I wanted to look at her forever, but Maverick spoke and ruined my fun.

"Was this your idea Bri? I remember you always mentioned you wished you could cook when we were younger," he said.

I didn't like his tone but kept my mouth shut.

Briar shook her head and leaned past me so she could look at him. "This was Scottie's idea actually. I gave up the idea of learning a long time ago, but he's convinced me it's a good skill to have."

"Girl I feel that! I never cared to learn either before Mav here, but he's gotten tired of take out. He convinced me this would be fun, and if it means he'll be happier if I cook for him than why not," Emily said with a smile.

That irked me. If she didn't care to learn, why did Maverick pressure her to do it? I was all for women making their own choices, and if she wanted to learn then good for her, but my judgement was permanently clouded when it came to that guy. Nothing could convince me he was a decent guy.

"I'm glad you like it!" Briar smiled.

"Good morning! My name is Kandee, and I'll be your instructor for today." Kandee was a small, older woman with purple hair and thin metal glasses. Her apron matched her hair and she had a serious demeanor about her. The reason I booked this class was because she used to work at one of the best restaurants in the city. She had skill and I wanted Briar to learn from the best.

Maverick leaned over as Kandee continued explaining what we'd be cooking for class, and I bristled at his attempt to push past me to Briar.

"She reminds me of Mrs. McMadden our junior year. You remember her?" he asked.

Briar let out a snort beside me and nodded her head. I placed my hand on the small of her back and a kiss on her head.

Kandee ended her instruction and Briar glanced up at me, a redness in her cheeks. I smiled as I grabbed the cutting board. "What's up? Nervous?"

"Only a lot. The last time I touched a vegetable I hurt myself," she said, holding up the asparagus.

I took it from her and placed it beside the garlic. "How about I cut and you cook. I'll walk you through the steps, and later on we can practice cutting. Does that sound okay?"

Something touched my shoulder and I peeked over to see Maverick smirking, his brow raised. "Careful with that one. She once tried to make me a birthday cake and almost caught her kitchen on fire."

I bit my tongue, now wasn't the time to tell him to fuck off, even though I wanted too. Instead, I was the bigger man and ignored him, smiling back at Briar who didn't seem to notice Maverick was talking out of his ass.

"That sounds perfect. Now, what should we do first?" she asked, a glimmer in those pretty blue eyes.

Briar wasn't a natural cook, but she was determined. Kandee left instructional cards on each table that included measurements, cooking temperatures, and detailed steps. By the time I'd finished chopping the asparagus, Briar had just finished measuring the seasonings for the steaks. She wiped the counter after every step and made sure there was enough room to work. It was hard to focus on helping her when the cute furrow between her brows was so distracting.

I watched silently as Briar kept an eye on the timer for the steak. It was almost done and I was so proud of her. She'd done it, from the seasoning to basting the steak was all Briar's doing. Her timer went off and she put it on the plate where the roasted asparagus had been waiting for ten minutes. It smelled delicious and I was excited to see how it turned out.

Beside us, Emily let out a moan when she ate their food, and Maverick didn't hide the smirk he threw my way. The dude thought he was better than us, than *me*.

Well, we were about to prove him wrong.

I didn't let the steak rest before I cut it with my knife. Briar was beside me, her eyes wide in anticipation as I took the first bite.

It was perfect. I dropped my utensils and threw my hands up, letting out a moan as the flavors covered my palate.

"It's good?" Briar asked with a worried smile.

I finished chewing and took a breath. "Baby this is the

best damn steak I've ever put in my mouth. Here." I cut a piece for her and held it out for her. "Try it."

She did and her face lit up as she smiled.

Maverick came to my side, fork in hand. "Can I try it? I want to make sure you guys aren't pulling my leg."

"Uh, no. First, this is ours. And second, Briar doesn't have to prove anything to you," I said, taking a step closer to him. It was a challenge. I didn't like how he talked about Briar, especially when she was right beside me.

"Scottie." Briar pulled on my sleeve. "Just ignore him."

I huffed and placed the rest of our food in the to-go container Kandee left on our table. Then I grabbed Briar's hand and smirked at Maverick. "Well this was fun. See you at work."

We walked out of the building and made it five feet before I felt Briar tug against me. I looked back and found her standing there, arms crossed, hip popped, and an eyebrow raised.

"Mind explaining what that was?" she asked.

briar

Scottie's brows furrowed as he rubbed the back of his neck, and I was wracking my brain trying to understand why he was so hostile toward Maverick. Sure, he deserved to be treated how he treaded others, but Scottie had turned into a colder version of himself I didn't recognize. He was short with Maverick, and he was never short with anyone.

At least in front of me he wasn't.

I dropped my shoulders and started walking past Scottie. As much as I wanted to have this conversation, we had to get home to take care of Mr. Moo. He couldn't be left alone for more than a couple hours, otherwise he was at risk of tearing off his diaper and pooping on everything.

Scottie dropped his head and walked beside me. "I don't like how he talks to you, especially after you told me how he treated you before."

"I never went into detail though, so for all you know you're making assumptions."

He shook his head. "You didn't have to say anything. I saw how you acted when you said he wasn't kind to you when you were together, and that itself is enough for me to not like him and honestly, I've been having problems with him at work. Both of those things clouded my judgement," he said.

I peered up at him. "Problems at work? What's he doing to you at work?"

As an equipment manager, I couldn't imagine Maverick was capable of causing problems. Had Scottie talked to my dad about it? How long had this been going on?

Scottie shook his head and grabbed my hand. "It's my problem to deal with. Everything is fine though, I'm sorry for not being on my best behavior."

I didn't doubt if he was being genuine, the way his brows creased and mouth tightened told me everything I needed to know. That despite a lifestyle of one-night stands and non-committal relationships, Scottie felt bad.

We reached his car, and he held my hand on the way home as I wondered what he was feeling. Was he always a jealous person? Or did he only act that way with certain people?

Mr. Moo was eager to see us when we got home, his diaper was intact thank goodness, and I took him outside to stretch his legs while Scottie put away the food we'd made. When I made it back inside, Scottie had laid out Mr. Moo's toys and potty pads in the living area. His nose scrunched when I put the dog down and he sneezed on Scottie's shoes.

"How long are you watching him again?" he asked.

"For the weekend. Why, do you not like dogs?" I asked.

Scottie eyed the old man and shoved his hands into his pockets. "I love dogs actually. But that one looks at me like he's plotting a murder. Maybe not mine, but someone's, and I feel like I should do something about it."

I laughed and walked into Scottie's open arms. "He's been like that since day one. Don't worry, he has no teeth and no opposable thumbs to do any harm."

He placed a kiss on the top of my head. "I hope you're right. Anyway, are you ready for next weekend?"

"What's next weekend?" I asked. I'd been so caught up with work and being wooed by Scottie that I'd forgotten most of the events I had scheduled in my calendar.

His hands dropped to the top of my butt and he grinned down at me. I loved looking at him when he smiled.

"The charity event. You know the one where I'll be auctioned off for a good cause?" He put a hand over his chest and sighed. "Oh how will all these old ladies react when they win?"

I stepped away from him and started for the stairs. "Be sure to remind them you're off the market while you're picking them off the floor from fainting with excitement."

"Are you getting jealous Clover?" Scottie asked, following after me with a sly grin.

I spun and continued up to his bedroom. When he walked in behind me and shut the door, I took off my bra and tossed it into an unknown corner. I'd find it later. Scottie's gaze was heated when I faced him, I crossed my arms to frustrate him.

"I think we both know that you're the jealous one between the two of us. What's up with that? I thought Mr. Bachelor would be immune to something like that."

His jaw clenched before he hid his warring emotions

with a smile. "That was old Scottie, new Scottie feels differently."

I sighed and laid back on his bed, making sure to stretch my arms so my shirt rode up to expose a little skin. "How does new Scottie feel?"

The bed dipped and a second later Scottie was hovering over me, his knee splitting my legs and leaving me suddenly aching for his touch.

"There's something you need to know Clover." He moved a strand of hair behind my ear and his brows held a tension I wanted to soothe away. "I know I'm not perfect, and I know that I can be a bit much for people, but none of those insecurities mattered until I met you. I went through life not thinking I was capable of feeling the things I feel for you, and I don't want to mess that up. But seeing Maverick, or any guy fighting me for your attention, it makes me mad."

Scottie leaned down, his lips were a breath away from mine before he moved to my ear. "You're all I think about, and I'll be damned if you're around another man without thinking about all the ways I make you come."

I arched against him, a silent plea for him to do something about the heat pooling in my stomach. "I might need a reminder before the charity event. After all, you won't be the only one in a suit, and likely not the only one fighting for—"

Scottie broke my sentence off with a demanding kiss, bringing his knee farther between my legs. I ground against him despite having little room, all while Scottie gripped the hair at the nape of my neck and pulled my mouth from him. His lips attacked my neck, nipping and sucking as he held me down.

"Don't talk about things like that," he said as he kissed my neck. "I should be the only one you think about."

"You've got an inflated ego." I gasped when he drew this thumb over my nipple. "I think about my vibrator too."

Scottie let out a low groan and pushed me farther into the mattress. "And I think about all the times I heard you through the walls."

The heat in my body intensified, but I wasn't blushing because I was turned on. I squirmed. "You heard me?"

"Mhm." He sat up and reached over to his nightstand, opening the drawer. "Got off to it too. More times than was appropriate if I'm being honest."

I watched as he pulled out something very purple and familiar from the drawer. The heat in my body zoned in on my stomach and I tried to sit up, but Scottie touched my chest and gently pushed me back down.

"Is that mine?" I asked.

He nodded and grinned wickedly. "I might have snooped the other night. I considered buying you a new one, but I know this is tried and true." He hit the button at the bottom, turning it on before he looked at me with a raised brow. "You okay?"

The only thing I could do was attempt to arch against him and was grateful he let me. Scottie grinned while he kissed me, I waited for him to put the vibrator at the apex of my thighs and gasped when he dragged it over my nipples. Back and forth in slow teasing movements. With his other hand, he unbuttoned my pants and only stopped kissing me to drag them down my thighs, leaving them half on.

I gasped as he kissed me, overwhelmed by the sensations teasing me and sending me over the edge.

"You're so beautiful Clover," Scottie said as he moved the vibrator to where I was aching between my legs. "Do you remember when I said we could test your theory about my bed being comfortable?"

My breath hitched as I remembered our text conversation. I was the first woman he'd brought into his bed, and it *was* comfortable. Damn him and his expensive mattress and soft sheets. He pressed the vibrator harder into my clit and I gripped the sheets.

"Is it living up to your expectations?" he asked, nipping my ear.

The only thing I could do was nod as my orgasm crashed through me. Scottie removed the vibrator and kissed my cheeks as I my head cleared. When I came too he had taken off his shirt. His hair was a tousled mess I wanted to grip now that I had free use of my hands. I lifted my hips as Scottie removed my jeans the rest of the way, then I was on him, tearing off his jeans and taking him into my mouth.

"Ah! Fuck." Scottie groaned as he bucked into my mouth.

I took my time like he did, licking and teasing the head of his cock slowly. His body kept bucking, a plea to go faster, go deeper, but I held out. This man couldn't tease me and take control without thinking I wouldn't do the same.

Scottie gripped my hair and pulled me off of him with a ragged moan.

"Top. Now," he said as he pulled me toward him. He placed his hands on my hips as I hovered over him. "Ride me. Please."

I loved hearing him say that word, maybe it was because in all other aspects of his life he took control. He was confident, a leader, so hearing him ask for something especially while he was beneath me set a fire in my veins. I lined his cock with my entrance and lowered myself onto him, I threw my head back as I felt the blissful stretch.

When I was fully seated, Scottie's grip tightened. His eyes were dark when I looked at him. "Hold on pretty girl."

That was all the warning I got before Scottie started to fuck me. The force of his hips sent me forward. Scottie wrapped his arms around me as he continued bucking his hips. The friction of his pelvis against mine, the fact I was trapped, it was all too much and it didn't take long until I was coming again. I bit into his shoulder as stars exploded behind my eyes and Scottie kissed my neck as he followed me over the edge shortly after.

When we were both spent, and I had gone to the bathroom, we laid in his bed. Scottie dragged his fingers over my back, my shirt forgotten on the floor, and he kissed my head.

"You've proven my theory right by the way," I said, looking up at him. His eyes were closed but he was smiling.

"Yeah?" he asked, his voice heavy with sleep.

I kissed his chest. "Yeah. This is the most comfortable bed I've ever been in."

scottie

Of all the things my father taught me; how to respect women, how to do all the maintenance on my car, and how to throw a wicked punch to protect my siblings, he never taught me how to tie a tie.

Yes, the internet was free, but I was determined to figure it out myself. How hard could it be to tie a piece of fabric together? I was so focused on my task in the mirror that I didn't notice Briar walk into the living room as I wrapped the larger piece around the small piece. Or was it the other way around?

"Need some help?" she asked.

I glanced up at her in the mirror and my breath caught in my throat. Slowly, I turned to face her and all the air in the room felt suffocating. Briar wore her hair in a high, slick back bun, leaving her neck exposed. A dainty gold pendant chain sat between her collarbones and her dress. There were no words.

The neckline hung tastefully low, not high enough to cover her chest but not low enough to worry about flashing anyone. The straps at her shoulders separated at the top, causing the split fabric to hang down to her knees. I couldn't drag my eyes from her as I looked her up and down.

"Scottie?" she asked again, blinking with those pretty blue eyes.

I stepped closer and reached out to grab her delicate hands. Linking our fingers together, I looked at her and smiled. "You're so beautiful."

Redness crept up her cheeks as she blinked at me. She licked her bottom lip, and I wished we didn't have to go. I wanted to bend Briar over the counter while she wore the dress, and spend all night buried between her thighs.

Maybe we could be fashionably late.

"Don't give me that look Scottie, you and I both know how important tonight is," she said with a pointed look, the redness gone.

"Okay but we can be a little late. No one's going to miss us,' I said, pulling her closer.

Briar grabbed the fabric across my shoulders and started assembling my tie. She shook her head. "Your team will miss you, and how bad would it look if you show up late for the auction? No, you're going to control yourself and we're leaving on time." She smoothed my tie and smiled up at me. "Got it?"

I nodded and gave her a quick kiss. "Got it. But the second we get home you're going over the edge of the couch." I glanced down and noticed the heels she wore. "And you're leaving those on."

I grabbed Briar's hand and led her out of the house, gave her a kiss as she got into the car, and then we were off. The charity event tonight was being held at an art museum, and I couldn't tell you why. I assumed it had to do with rich people liking art, but that was only a guess. I grabbed Briar's leg as I drove, she tapped away at her phone with a smile.

"What's got you excited?" I asked.

She looked at me and spoke with excitement in her voice. "Last week my dad introduced me to someone who works at the network. She emailed me about a possible internship with her."

Briar's blog had really taken off since working with the team, and had accumulated a decent following of people who weren't into hockey. There was something about the way she wrote that made sports jargon easy and fun to understand. I was immensely proud of her. I squeezed her leg again.

"That's awesome, maybe she'll be at the event tonight and you two can chat more about it."

Briar nodded. "Yeah maybe, but honestly, I'd rather hang off your arm for as long as I can. That sounds more fun. Work can wait another day."

The museum had a red carpet laid out at the entrance and a valet service—fancy. I handed my keys to the older gentleman who was dressed in a black button-up and dark jeans, and stopped another younger man from opening Briar's door. That was my job. I held Briar's hand as we made our way past a few photographers and into the museum. Classical music played as people chatted amongst themselves, all dressed in elegant clothing.

A server approached us offering refreshments, but I only cared about the food.

Briar and I walked toward the crowd, and I scanned the area for my friends. All of Denver's professional sports teams were in attendance tonight so it took a moment for me to find Case. He and Basil were standing at a table, drinks in hand. It was Basil who spotted us first.

"Finally! You two made it," she said with a grin as we approached her.

Her and Briar hugged while I gave Case a pat on the back. "Fancy seeing you in a suit," he said.

"I fill it out pretty well, don't you think?" I asked with a spin, turning toward the girls. "And you look stunning tonight, Basil."

She smiled and placed her hands on her hips. Her dress was a deep purple and strapless, her hair flowed in soft curls down her back. "Thank you, Scottie. You look very handsome and might I add your tie looks too perfect. Is it a clip on?"

Briar and I laughed as she came to stand at my side. "Don't insult my girlfriend like that, it's not very nice."

Basil smiled at Case, and I grabbed Briar's waist, pulling her more into my side. Briar cleared her throat. "So what's the charity for? Scottie never said."

Case adjusted his bow tie. "So the attendees have the option to pick a charity to donate to. They haven't announced the charities yet though, that'll come with the auction."

"Oh. Are you auctioning yourself tonight?" Briar asked.

He nodded. "Yes, Scottie, Riley and I were the only ones on the team who volunteered for it."

A server walked by us and I grabbed us two small quiches from the plate. She eagerly took a bite before Basil grabbed her hand and whispered something in her ear. They walked away, leaving Case and I alone.

"So. Girlfriend huh?" he asked when the girls were far enough away."

I downed the rest of my champagne. "You heard that right. She's mine and I'm never letting her go."

I thought of all the things we could do; travel across Europe, pick up a millennial hobby like train for a marathon or get into sourdough. I was staying for all of it.

"Good evening, everyone, thank you for being here tonight."

There was an older man at the front of the room, dressed in a dark green suit and had a handlebar mustache. He went through thanking the guests and giving a speech about the event before he announced the first auction. As he spoke, the servers went around and handed slips to the guests, on it was a list of various charities to donate your funds to when you won an auction item.

The girls came back while he rambled. With drinks in hand, I tucked Briar back into my side. I leaned down and whispered, "You need to win the bid for a date with me."

"Why?" she asked.

"Because my money will go to a good cause, and I don't want to dance with someone's grandma when you're right here."

"Would our volunteers for our first auction please make their way to the front of the room?" the man said.

I gave Briar a quick kiss before Case and I made our way up. Riley met us there and grinned. "Hey! Didn't see you guys, glad you could both make it."

"You didn't see us because you were probably busy trying to get someone's number," I said, putting my hands in my pockets.

The auction started, and as the man listed our names

and other information from a form we filled out months ago, I looked for Briar. She and Basil sat toward the back of the crowd. I never looked away from her as the auction started. They auctioned Case off first and an older woman in her sixties won the bidding. I wasn't sure how Basil felt about it, but that was between the happy couple.

"And here we have Scottie Lancaster. A forward for the Denver Peaks. He's twenty-seven, enjoys cooking and long hikes. Who would like to start the bidding at five-thousand dollars?"

Various women held up their cards, but I didn't notice them, not when Briar winked at me before holding up her own card. She held it up as the bid went higher and higher, and I did my best to wide my widening grin, not caring about the hit to my bank account.

"Fifty thousand going once, twice, *sold* to number thirty-one."

I grinned as Briar lowered her card and tried not to look at the disappointment on some of the women's faces as I walked toward the crowd. Briar grinned as I approached her, she threw her arms over my shoulders when I reached her.

"Hey," she said.

"You won me at auction. I owe you a date," I said as I pulled her in closer. My nose grazed the top of her head, taking in that perfect coconut smell. I was tempted to leave early, or at least leave the building so I could show her just how much I was looking forward to our *date.*

But then we were interrupted by the last person I wanted to see. Maverick.

"Fancy seeing you guys here," he said with a smile. Emily was on his arm, her hair curled and pinned back behind her ears. For some reason her hair looked different, less vibrant than the last time we saw her, but I couldn't tell why. "Briar, you look fantastic."

"Way to compliment someone else's date," I said with a smile. "Now if you don't mind, I owe her a dance."

Maverick stood straighter. "A guy can't give an old friend a compliment?" he asked.

"You can. But considering you're exes and you're here with your own date, it just seems a little distasteful. Don't you think?" I asked.

Briar stepped away from me and faced Maverick. "I think you should pay more attention to your date than spending your time and energy seeking me out."

His mouth morphed into a tense line before he nodded and walked away with Emily, who looked as uncomfortable as I felt. Seriously, what did she see in that guy? My phone buzzed in my pocket and I glanced at the caller ID and silenced it.

"Who's that?" Briar asked with a tilt of her head.

"My sister, but it's not important. Now how about that dance?" I grabbed Briar's hand, but my phone buzzed again.

Briar smiled. "We have all night, see what she needs."

Damn little sisters and their cock blocking ways.

"Hey sis," I said, my voice a little more clipped than it needed to be.

"Uh hey." Her voice seemed unsteady. "I kinda need your help with something," she said.

My stomach dropped and I gave Briar a panicked look. There had only been one other time my youngest sister had called me sounding like her world was ending.

"What's wrong? Is everything okay?" I asked, dragging Briar out of the museum and toward the valet attendant.

"I'm okay, not hurt or anything. But I need you to pick me up from the airport."

There was something off about her tone, it didn't hold the anxiety I thought I heard earlier. Briar and I got into the car and I gripped the steering wheel.

"Katie, why are you at the airport?"

"I moved to Denver. Surprise."

briar

Katie Lancaster and her brother shared a lot of similarities; the angle of her jaw, the bridge of her nose, and her freckles. The only differences they had were, she was blonde and had brown eyes. Despite those two differences I half expected them to share the same personality, that was what happened when you had siblings right? They grew up in the same house, raised by the same people, and surely Scottie had some influence on her as her older brother.

I was so far from wrong I didn't think I'd be right about anything ever again.

We picked Katie up from the airport an hour ago and while it made me a little upset to miss a dance with Scottie, I was relieved that his sister was fine.

Or was. She was currently being reamed out by Scottie while I watched with popcorn in my lap. I couldn't tell if I was happy or not that I didn't have siblings. This was mildly entertaining.

"What do you mean you didn't tell Mom and Dad you moved halfway across the country? You just up and left with all your shit?" Scottie asked, running a hand through his hair.

His sister shrugged as if it wasn't a huge deal she lied to her parents.

"I'm an adult who can do what I want, and you're acting like I ghosted them. I texted them two weeks ago that I was moving here for a culinary program, it's not my responsibility to make sure they read their texts," she said.

"You didn't think to follow up with them? Katie, you're the youngest and have left our parents as empty nesters without sufficient warning. Mom never made you your last dinner did she? Wow, okay." Scottie pinched the bridge of his nose and took three deep breaths all while Kaite stared at him. "Here's the deal. Tonight, I'm going to call them and tell them you made it here safe. Tomorrow morning you're calling them to apologize about how you left."

"Why don't I call them right now?" she asked.

"Because they're both going to be mad and I've got to calm them down. Trust me, if you talked to them they'd feel the need to come out here and deal with you face-to-face. Is that what you want?"

I ate more popcorn, needing to ask Scottie about his family lore. Because from what little he told me that night we cooked together, I assumed they were your typical happy family. Was I wrong?

Katie picked at the skin on her thumb for a minute before letting out a heavy sigh. "Fine," she said.

She grabbed her suitcase and walked upstairs without a bid goodnight. Scottie loosened his tie and sighed before walking toward me. I moved so he could sit next to me, but instead he dropped to his knees, wrapped his arms around my hips and laid his head in my lap. The position didn't look comfortable with his large frame and the muscles that seemed to have gotten bigger this season, so I did something I thought would make him more comfortable.

I ran my fingers through his hair and offered a piece of popcorn.

"Be grateful you don't have siblings, they're a handful," he said.

"Is it too soon to ask what all that was about? Is she in trouble?"

Scottie shook his head and peered up at me. "Our parents are the definition of overprotective, and Kaite can be a bit impulsive and doesn't always think about other people's feelings. It's not that she doesn't care, she just processes things differently. Anyway, I know they don't care that she's moving for whatever culinary thing she's doing. They care that she's being too impulsive and hasn't thought everything through."

I scratched his scalp again, tugging on his hair every so often. "Are you worried about her?"

He thought about it for a moment, his fingers dragging over the silk fabric of my dress. "Not really. She's impulsive but she isn't stupid. I wouldn't put it past her to have set up living arrangements a week or so before she moved out here."

Scottie sat up and smiled, his eyes heavy and his expression not as carefree as I loved. "Let's go to bed, we can talk about this more tomorrow."

He stood and held out his hand which I took without hesitation. Butterflies swarmed in my stomach with the touch, but they felt different somehow. Before when he smiled at me, touched me or made me laugh, the flutters were soft. They traveled from my stomach to my chest to all of my extremities, but this flutter made its way to my chest and stayed there.

Looking back, I knew this wasn't the first time it'd happened, but it's the first time I really paid attention to what it might mean.

———

Scottie was in the kitchen when I walked downstairs, shirt off, pajamas hanging low on his hips and I bit my lap at the memory of last night. We went to bed *very* late and yet he looked like he got a full night's rest.

Chocolate chip pancakes were stacked on a large plate, along with eggs and sausage. I made two plates, one for me and the other for Scottie. We were halfway through breakfast when Katie came downstairs.

Her hair was in a neat braid down her back and she smiled at both of us. "Morning!"

Scottie made a noncommittal noise as he kept eating and I chalked it up to him being upset with his sister for the position she put him in. I wondered if he had already called their parents or not.

Kaite made her plate and sat next to me. She turned and held out her hand. "We never really had a proper introduction. I'm Katie, and I'm sorry for how last night went. That wasn't the best first impression."

"You're sucking up to her because you know she can make me be nice to you," Scottie said as he stabbed a sausage.

Katie rolled her eyes. "You're always nice to me. Last night was a bad attempt at you being mad and you know it."

"I held back because we had company." Scottie pointed

at her with his fork, his brows were furrowed as if he was serious, but it seemed too forced.

"Yeah, yeah if that makes you feel better then keep believing it," Kaite said with a smirk.

I took her hand and laughed. "Nice to officially meet you. I'm Briar, not sure if my name got lost in the circumstances last night or not."

Scottie's phone rang from the counter and he let out a heavy sigh as he stood from the table. He gave Katie a pointed look. "If they disown me for harboring a fugitive it's your fault." He put the phone to his ear. "Hey Mama."

We watched as Scottie left the kitchen, and when a door in the distance shut, Katie faced me, a sly smirk playing on her face. "I need to know everything about how you got my brother to settle down."

I choked on an egg and downed my orange juice so I could live to see another day. "What do you mean?"

She pulled out her phone. "I'm not privy to my brothers dating life outside of what I see online. Because, ew. Anyways the past couple months every time he pops up on my feed it's a picture of you two together. His last longest streak of being photographed with a woman was three days. So I need to know if you're visiting for the major holidays, and if you are, I need sizes so I can make you stuff. Last year my sister and I did quilt sweater things."

It was a little jarring to be invited by this woman I just met to her family gatherings when Scottie and I hadn't even discussed it. When I didn't answer, her brows creased together and she leaned in.

"You two are together, aren't you? Or is this one of those fake arrangements I read about in my books?"

Heat crawled up my cheeks and Katie's eyes widened.

She slammed a hand down and stood from the table. "I *knew* it! My brother's a total whore." She lowered her voice and leaned in. "Do you need help? Is this a contract thing you have to break or a vocal agreement? Either way I can help, blink twice if you need my help."

I made a point to not blink and nearly gave myself dry eye as I tried to gather my thoughts. These two were more alike than I thought.

"No. Well, kind of?" I shook my head and blinked, but kept my head down so she didn't think I was trying to signal I needed to be rescued. I chuckled. "It started off that way, but I promise you we are very much a real thing and I'm very happy."

Katie's eyes narrowed for a second. "You're positive?"

I nodded. "More positive than I've been about anything else in my life."

"Okay good." She sat down and stabbed her fork into her eggs. "Now tell me about how you two met. Scottie's going to make the story weird and short, he's a dude and you know how they leave out important details."

Yeah there was no way I was going to tell his sister we had a one-night stand. So I went for the cleaner story. "My dad is his coach, and I was offered as a sacrifice to help his image in exchange for being able to do a piece on his team for my job. It was a win-win, and at some point it stopped being fake."

Katie nodded along and when she looked at me again I could see the genuine concern she had. "And you're sure he makes you happy? I might not ask about his dating life, but again, I see what's said about my brother online. I don't want either of you to get hurt."

Scottie walked back into the kitchen, now fully

clothed much to my dismay, and walked over to Katie and pinched her ear.

"Ow!" She smacked his hand.

"It's what you get. Mom and Dad made me promise to keep tabs on you while you're in town and send them updates. Do you know how hard that's going to be when you suck at texting *and* I have Briar to devote all my extra attention to?"

As Scottie kept rambling, Katie smiled at me, seeming to understand that I meant what I said about being happy. And I think she realized that Scottie was happy too.

scottie

Failure was inevitable in all facets of life, but it's how you acted after failure that mattered most. And I was self-aware enough that I did not take failure well, especially when it wasn't my fault. I think that was why I stormed straight to the equipment room after our game, with Case trailing after me.

I didn't notice there was an issue with my skates until I was thrown into rotation during the second period. They kept catching on the small scratches in the ice, threatening to send me tumbling into the ice or toward my teammates, and there was only one other person who ever touched my skates.

Maverick.

I didn't know what the dude's problem was, between the comments he made toward Briar on our double date, to how he seemed to pressure her for attention at the charity event, to earlier this week when he tried to give her a hug. He might not have seen how her body tensed, but I did, and it was why I removed him from Briar. I didn't punch him—I should have—but I did tell him to keep his hands to himself.

My skates though. That was the last straw because not only was he not doing his job, but he was intentionally putting me and everyone else on the ice at risk. Have you ever tripped and body slammed into another six-foot-something man who weighed two hundred plus pounds?

It wasn't fun.

"Scottie! Leave it be," Case said as I entered the equipment room.

Maverick was busy packing up his work bag, he didn't seem as upset as I expected. We were no longer in the playoffs due to his mistake, which would make anyone on the team upset. Hell, our social media manager had an entire folder of content ideas from now until we inevitably won. It was all going to waste and he was to blame.

He turned toward us and crossed his arms. "I'm surprised to see you here, Lancaster. I would have thought you'd be crying in Briar's arms or drowning your sorrows with beer. Or you know, be hitting on someone at a dingy bar."

Case sucked in a breath beside me. "What is your problem?"

"Yeah. What the fuck dude? You've been a pain in my ass since Briar's been in town."

Maverick rolled his eyes and crossed his arms. "Are you kidding me? Do you really not know?"

Case and I looked at each other and I shrugged. "No clue, please enlighten me."

Maverick leaned back against his littered desk; skates, athletic tape, and gloves were piled on top, and I couldn't help but be annoyed by his lack of organizational skills.

He crossed his arms and stared at us with a tight expression. "Everyone knows you and Briar are faking it. Did you think the team wouldn't figure out that your lifestyle caught up with you and you needed to be bailed out by Warner?"

I could admit that sleeping around with women publicly wasn't the best choice I'd ever made, but Maverick wasn't in a position to say anything. We weren't friends, I never hurt anyone, least of all him.

"What's it to you?" I asked.

"Seriously? You think I'm going to let you cock block me from talking to Briar when your relationship isn't even real?" he asked.

Case shifted on his feet next to me and I wondered if he felt the same anger in my chest when he was going through the stuff with his ex a couple years ago. Did he feel angry that his problem wouldn't leave him alone?

I threw my hands out. "Cock block? Dude, how have you not gotten the hint that she's not interested in interacting with you? She told me she didn't even want to go on the double date with you. So maybe go look in the mirror if you can't find the problem with this whole thing."

He clicked his tongue. "Come on. It's been years since we've seen each other. I'm sure her feelings have changed. We're different people now."

Case put his hand on my shoulder to keep me from walking forward. "Don't you have a girlfriend?" he asked.

Emily didn't deserve this fucker, especially when he was pushing to get on his ex-girlfriend's good side.

Maverick shrugged. "She couldn't get over the fact I wanted to be friends with Briar again, so we called things off."

We stared at him. How could he be so heartless and dense as to go after another taken woman when he was in a relationship. The more he opened his mouth, the more angry I got, and I was grateful Case still had a hold of me.

"Anyway, now that you've done your little PR thing, you should be done with her right? Think you can convince her to get coffee with me?" Maverick asked. "You know, since you're done putting on the boyfriend charade? Taking my hand off her was a good show by the way. You play into the jealous boyfriend thing really well."

There was half a second where my subconscious was able to whisper *it's a bad idea.* But it wasn't fast enough to keep me from walking across the room and punching Maverick in his face. His head snapped back and when he looked at me again, his nose was bloody and his eyes were bloodshot.

"What the fuck!" he yelled before charging me.

His arms wrapped around my mid-section. Before he managed to push me back, he landed a punch at my side, but all it did was anger me more. I had a good twenty pounds on him and a couple inches. He shouldn't have been able to push me back.

I shoved him off of me and in the midst of getting my footing again, he swung and landed a punch on my jaw. The pain didn't register before I punched him back. I wasn't sure how long the fight lasted, minutes or seconds, but there were arms around my shoulders pulling me back.

There was also a lot of yelling from one person I didn't want to see.

"Lancaster!" Coach Warner yelled.

I shoved off whoever was holding me back and saw that Riley still had a grip on Maverick. Blood dripped down his face and his right eye was starting to shut. I knew I couldn't look much better than him. Case came to my side, his mouth tight as he directed my shoulders toward the door.

It was time to leave and there was no room for negotiation.

Case, Coach, and I walked out of the room. I followed behind them as we made our way back to the locker room. Everyone else had gone home—the fans, the reporters and it was eerily quiet when I sat on the bench and put my head in my hands.

My head hurt like a motherfucker, but it was worth it to knock some sense into Maverick. If he tried to continue to make a move on Briar, I'd hit him again and harder to get it through his thick skull that she wasn't ever going to want him again. I wasn't going to sit by while the woman I loved was being harassed.

There were hushed voices for a while, then silence for longer than I kept track of. Why was Coach keeping me here? Was he talking to Maverick first?

That liar, he'd probably say I went after him first and would claim innocence. The door opened and I had my story laid out for Coach, but when I glanced up it wasn't him who stood in front of me.

It was Briar.

briar

Right after the game...

Katie was shouting at her brother when he tripped again and missed a pass from Riley, and I cowered away from her for fear that she'd yell at me too.

Danny leaned in and whispered, "Scottie's sister is terrifying."

I nodded and finished off my beer, keeping an eye on Scottie below. There was something very wrong with how he was playing, and I wanted to go ask my dad about it, but he was too far and I knew he didn't need to answer my questions. I'd wait until after the game because Scottie was going to need time to cool off before I talked to him.

Katie spun toward us and when the other team scored, she threw her arms out. "What is up with him! He's out there like a chicken with its head cut off!"

She spun back to the game and Danny looked at me, he spun his finger around the side of his head, and I smacked him. The rest of the game was the same, Scottie struggling to find his footing and me wondering why my dad didn't pull him. There were a couple other guys who could easily take his place, sure they weren't as good, but they were there for instances like this.

The final buzzer rang and my heart dropped at the score. The Peaks lost, that was it for the season.

Katie groaned and kicked some popcorn that had fallen to the ground and Danny stretched his arms over his head, making sure to show off the new gold jewelry on his left ring finger. He'd gotten engaged on that weekend trip and I was ecstatic for him. I'd also been wrangled into wedding planning which I couldn't get out of because I was deeply convinced no one else could put their wedding together.

"So much for a great game!" Kaite sat down and crossed her arms. "The first game I see him play in person and they lose," she grumbled.

I put my hand on her leg and smiled. "Hey, it happens. I'm sure he's still happy you were here regardless."

She shrugged. "You're right. Let's go find him. Knowing how he gets after a loss, he could use the support. Lancasters are overly competitive to a fault."

Danny raised a brow. "I couldn't tell."

I shook my head and followed behind the two of them, my mind wandered to every possibility of why Scottie played like that. Tripping over nothing, slamming into other players without cause. By the time we made it out of the arena most everyone had left, and I was ready to say good night to Danny when my dad came around a corner, his shoulders held back as he stared at me.

"Uh, can you stay with her?" I asked Danny. I felt horrible leaving Katie by herself in a new place, but it was obvious my dad needed me. He used to look like that growing up; I'd come home from school and he'd have to talk to me about a grade, or he'd tell me something happened to a family member. He looked like that when he told me about the divorce.

Danny nodded and I made my way toward my dad with my head held high. What could he possibly need to tell me?

He held out his arm and I walked into his embrace before he directed me toward the hallway. He took in a deep breath, and I remained silent.

"I heard some very interesting information just now," he said as we continued walking. "And I'd like to hear what you have to say before I make any rash decisions."

We stopped in the middle of the hallway, far enough from prying ears if there were any. Dad leaned against the wall and crossed his arms while I clenched my fists. He cleared his throat.

"I was told that you and Lancaster have decided to make your arrangement more permanent."

Shit. He found out, but how? I was still coming up with a plan to break the news to him—it involved revisiting that diner that got us in this situation. The last thing I wanted to do was keep secrets from my dad, but I didn't want to tell him anything if it wasn't serious. Scottie and I were still figuring out our new relationship and the last thing I wanted to do was tell my dad only for it to not work out.

I nodded. "We had a conversation a few weeks ago. Dad I—"

He held up a hand, cutting me off. "I was also told that you and Maverick have been having problems?"

It was hard to deny that Maverick had been pushing

boundaries, both mine and Scottie's. So I nodded and glanced at the ground. "Yes."

"Why didn't you tell me?" he asked.

I bit my bottom lip. "Because I didn't want my complaints to come across as me being entitled or me thinking I have power or whatever because I'm your daughter."

He shook his head. "You'd never come across that way, hon. The guys all know you're not here to cause problems. I do wish you told me, but I'm also happy you have someone in your corner to stand up for you."

My brows furrowed. "What are you talking about?"

Dad tilted his head, a command to follow him. We turned a corner, and I realized quickly that we were headed toward the locker rooms. We got to the door and he pulled me into a hug. "While I wish you kept me in the loop, I understand that's just not who you are. Cut the guy some slack when you get in there okay? He's had a rough night."

He walked off before I had the chance to ask what he was talking about. The door to the locker room was unlocked and I wasn't expecting what was inside. Scottie sat on a bench with his head low, but even at the obscure angle I could see the bruise forming on his face. My breath caught when he lifted his head, he had a cut in his eyebrow and another bruise on his temple.

"What happened?" I asked, rushing toward him. I placed my hands on either side of his face, careful not to put too much pressure, and Scottie kissed my palm. "Did this happen during the game?"

He shook his head. "After. You should see Maverick."

"I need you to explain before my mind thinks of the

worst thing possible," I said, my eyes scanning him to make sure I wasn't missing anything.

He grabbed my wrist as if to brace himself. "He was being a dick and said some things about you that aren't worth repeating. He also didn't sharpen my skate on purpose, that's why I played like ass."

"How do you know it was on purpose?" I asked.

Scottie kissed my palm again. "He asked for my skates earlier this week to sharpen and said they were good to go before the game. I didn't have time to fix them, and he only gave me one pair back. I didn't realize it until I got on the ice."

Anger bloomed in my chest. Maverick intentionally let Scottie go onto the ice with dull skates? That was danger-ous, Scottie was lucky he hadn't hurt himself or someone else.

"So did you beat him up for you or for me?" I asked, trying to deflect from how I felt. I was tempted to find Maverick and punch him too, but I wouldn't do as much damage as Scottie did, so I'd leave him alone. For now.

Scottie looked at me with those blue eyes I loved so much and winked. "Can't let anyone talk bad about the woman I love. There's no excuse, and I will defend you every single time."

Love.

Something I wasn't expecting to feel when I looked at him, when he made me laugh or made me smile. It was inevitable though, to fall in love with someone when neither of us were looking for it.

I kissed him and was careful to keep from climbing in his lap. "I love you too, Hot Shot."

Air whooshed out of him and his hands dropped to my waist. We kissed for a while, long enough to make me anxious about my dad or staff walking in on us. That was the only reason I pulled away from him.

I held out my hand. "Let's go home."

He stopped me from turning from him and pulled me into a hug. He was warm, sweaty, and I was certain he was sore. He nuzzled his nose into my hair, and his chest expanded with an inhale.

"Do you think your dad will still buy you a house considering how everything turned out?"

I huffed a laugh and held him tighter. "As if you can't buy us a new one on your own?"

"I'm not going to turn down a free house if I don't have too," he said. We plummeted back into silence and I was acutely aware of the dwindling noises outside of the room. People were leaving and they were going to start getting ready to close the building soon.

"Scottie? We need to go before we get locked in here."

"Locked in here or under the covers, you're my home. So I don't care to move from this spot too much."

I shook my head and turned my head into his chest. Scottie was my home too and I never wanted to be anywhere else.

epilogue

Scottie

2 years later…

The doorbell rang, startling the old German shepherd from his afternoon nap. He rushed toward the front room with Briar calling after him.

A second later Hayley rushed into the large living room—my favorite part of the new house—with Max, the dog, right behind her. He barked in excitement as she flew into my arms.

"Hi Uncle Scottie!" She smiled, her braces now decorated with a neon green band. Apparently they were starting to put braces on kids younger and younger. There was a reason behind it but I never remembered.

Instead I always noted the new color, then moved on with my day.

Townes and a very pregnant Hollis wandered in, and the poor dude looked like he was going to pass out from stress. His scowl was deeper as he watched Hollis waddle to the couch, her bag over his shoulder.

I looked at Hayley. "When did you get so big?"

She shook her head before separating herself to make friends with my pantry. Briar sat next to Hollis on the couch, her wedding ring shimmering in the light.

"How are you feeling?" she asked.

Hollis sighed. "Ready for this kiddo to be here, everything hurts, I can't eat more than three bites of anything, and Townes here is acting like a mother hen." He cleared his throat, and she smiled at him. "Sorry babe, but it's true."

Townes looked at me as he placed Hollis's purse on the island. "When are Case and Basil showing up?"

I glanced at my phone and sighed when I didn't see any new messages. "An hour ago they said an hour. So hopefully soon unless they got a flat tire in the mountains and have no signal."

Briar spun her head toward us. "Hey! Don't stress out the pregnant lady."

Hollis whispered something to her which made her laugh.

Hayley walked over with a bag of chips. "Can I take Max around the property Uncle T?"

Townes nodded. "Don't go too far, it's still icy outside."

Last year Briar and I decided to spend Thanksgiving in Breckinridge, and at the time it sounded like a great idea. We booked an Airbnb and invited our friends to celebrate. That was before we discovered that Hollis was expecting and that Case and Basil were going to start trying soon.

Which, we all knew what that meant, but I was proud of myself for not making a joke. The last two weeks I'd been anxious about my friends making it up and now that they were here, it hadn't gotten any better.

Briar walked toward me and slid her hand into my back pocket. "You okay?"

"What if Hollis goes into labor? Will she have to be life flighted or something?" I asked. I had other nephews and nieces, but I'd never been around for the births. A text message would hit my phone in the middle of the night announcing the newest family member and I'd call the next morning to give my congratulations.

Hollis was the closest pregnant person I'd been around, and for a second I wondered if I was feeling what Townes did.

Briar grabbed my hand and smiled. "Let's go outside real quick."

I followed her, unable to say no to my wife.

I was still getting used to calling her that. We got married six months ago, long enough that you'd think you'd get used to the new title. But I never wanted to get used to it, calling her my wife was the greatest gift I was given and I was going to treasure it until the day we died. Sometimes I couldn't believe where we started. From an arrangement set up by her dad, to married and very much in love.

It was perfect.

We walked to the edge of the property and Briar spun toward me, placing her hands over my shoulders, we started swaying. She liked to dance with me every chance we got. She said I was still making it up to her from the charity event when we left early.

Katie finished culinary school and was now a contestant on a TV show, so I would say it was a little worth it to leave and get her from the airport that night.

"What's on your mind?" Briar asked, pulling at the hair at the base of my skull.

My hands gripped her waist tighter. "I'm just thinking about us. How I got so lucky to call you mine forever."

Also how proud I was of my wife for securing her dream job working as a sportswriter for the network, she was starting after the holidays. I thought about how lucky I was I still had a job. That night I went after Maverick was horrible, I was put on suspension while Maverick was investigated for the things I claimed. Not only about my skates, but for how he treated Briar. He ended up getting fired for endangering an athlete and I was forced to pay a fine for misconduct.

It was worth it to not deal with him ever again.

She smiled up at me and my heart constricted in my chest. I kissed her quickly and spun her. When she came back into my arms, I held her hand over my heart.

"Have I ever told you why the nickname stuck? Clover?"

She shook her head. "No, but I'm curious now."

I looked at her blue eyes and almost drowned in the blues that held my heart. "It's because I didn't believe in luck until I met you. You're my special Clover and I'm going to keep calling you that until my luck runs out and then some."

Her breath hitched and I was going to kiss her again, but a familiar voice shouted from behind us.

"Hey we made it—oh! Sorry. Keep being in love and

shit. We'll be inside," Case said as he walked toward the house.

Briar and I laughed and as much as I wanted to stay here with her forever, we had the rest of our lives to continue to be in love. So we walked inside, hand in hand, and I couldn't help but think of the new ways I'd love her tomorrow, and every day after that.

www.ingramcontent.com/pod-product-compliance
Lightning Source LLC
Chambersburg PA
CBHW032244310726
48973CB00008B/2293